"I w[on't let you go]
without an explanation"

There was no anger in Adam's voice, just ice-cold determination. "Why did you leave me, Rochelle?"

She knew that he only wanted information. Why it mattered after all this time she didn't know. Pride perhaps? Or was it revenge?

"You listen to me for once," she cried. "I escaped your selfishness and manipulation once, and I'll do it again. I don't need you, Adam Trelawney. I don't need anyone!" Her hand clutched the door to her cottage and to safety.

"Just one more thing," he said. He seized her shoulders, pulling her roughly against him, his mouth descending on hers in a forceful kiss that crushed her lips.

With a wordless moan she clung to him. She knew this was what she'd yearned for. Hostility and apprehension melted away. Was it love she was feeling?

Dana James lives with her husband and three children in a converted barn on the edge of a Cornish village. She has written thrillers, historical and doctor-nurse romances but is now concentrating her efforts on writing contemporary romance fiction. In addition to extensive researching, which she adores, the author tries to write for at least four hours every day.

Books by Dana James

HARLEQUIN ROMANCE
2632—DESERT FLOWER
2841—THE MARATI LEGACY
2872—THE EAGLE AND THE SON

Don't miss any of our special offers. Write to us at the following address for information on our newest releases.

Harlequin Reader Service
901 Fuhrmann Blvd., P.O. Box 1397, Buffalo, NY 14240
Canadian address: P.O. Box 603,
Fort Erie, Ont. L2A 5X3

Heart
of Glass
Dana James

Harlequin Books

TORONTO • NEW YORK • LONDON
AMSTERDAM • PARIS • SYDNEY • HAMBURG
STOCKHOLM • ATHENS • TOKYO • MILAN

Original hardcover edition published in 1987
by Mills & Boon Limited

ISBN 0-373-17005-X

Harlequin Romance first edition January 1988

CHAPTER ONE

ADAM TRELAWNEY lifted the newly installed telephone from a large plan spread out on the floor of the empty room and set it on the marble hearth.

Rolling the plan into its protecting cardboard tube, he straightened with athletic ease, and brushed dust from the sleeve of his beautifully cut business suit.

He stood a little over six feet, but the finely patterned dark cloth made him appear even taller. A pale blue shirt and striped tie emphasised the blackness of thick, wavy hair curling crisply on his neck.

Cloud-grey eyes beneath straight black brows surveyed the room. Its beautiful proportions were repeated throughout the house.

Late-afternoon sunlight streamed in through long, elegant windows, the cracked and missing panes now replaced. Even the cobwebs, dust and years of neglect could not detract from the high moulded ceiling and white marble fireplace.

The decorators had started outside. Interior work would begin tomorrow, and once that was finished, the hardwood floor, now muddy and dirt-streaked, would again reveal its mellow beauty.

Absently turning the plan in his hands, Adam moved to the window. It would take longer to restore the gardens. He had already begun to ask around, trying to find the men who used to work here. Knowing the soil and the needs of the plants, shrubs and trees that grew in it, he considered they would need little supervision. And with the money he was prepared to pay, the work would be done willingly. His chiselled mouth, with its slightly fuller lower lip, quirked cynically. But as he lifted his gaze to the town on the far side of the river, his eyes were bleak and cold.

Turning abruptly, he left the house, locking the front door behind him. His footsteps crunched on the weed-choked gravel. As he approached the maroon Daimler it occurred to him that he would have to buy another car. Something smaller and more suited to the narrow, winding Cornish roads. He'd keep the Daimler though; it would be useful for trips up to London.

He got into the car, tossed the plan on to the back seat, and glanced out of the side window at the house. His mouth twisted in self-mockery.

What was he doing here? Why had he bought this place? He had washed his hands of her, put her out of his mind—*over and over again.* She had walked—no, run—out of his life without a word of explanation, and had it not been for the strange business of Nicholas's will, it was unlikely their paths would ever have crossed again.

The car-phone beeped softly. He lifted the receiver. 'Trelawney.' He listened. 'No, not this afternoon. It will have to be tomorrow.' He turned his head and his gaze focused on a row of four terraced cottages on the quay almost directly opposite. 'I have a meeting.' He listened again. 'Important? It could be,' he said quietly and replaced the receiver. His long, powerful fingers lingered for a moment on the cool plastic, his expression brooding.

Then his jaw tightened, jutting stubbornly. One corner of his mouth tilted in a grim smile, and with the self-assurance that characterised all his actions he started the big car and, at the top of the curving drive, turned on to the road which would take him across the bridge and into the town.

* * *

Setting her suitcase down, Shelley glanced round, heaving a happy sigh. The soft jade green of the rough-plastered walls was echoed in the short-piled carpet. The sofa and armchair she had re-covered in a Sanderson print of rose, cream and grey, faced the open fireplace. Alcoves on either side contained her books, a compact stereo unit and rose-shaded lamps. Her tiny portable TV stood on a table in the corner. All just as she had left it. It was good to be home.

She scooped up the letters scattered on the mat and, with barely a cursory glance, laid them on the small, polished table below the narrow staircase. She had all evening to read them, though no doubt most of them would be invoices or bills.

Her first and most important task was to get some food in, then light a fire and air the cottage. She had been away only a fortnight, but March had poked cold, damp fingers into every corner.

Collecting her shopping basket and purse, Shelley went out once more into the late-afternoon sunlight. Scanning the harbour, she revelled in the familiar and much-loved view.

A stiff breeze stirred the water into choppy waves tipped with white foam. The workboats were back on their moorings, sails stowed, having returned from dredging for oysters in the estuary.

Tangerine and shocking-pink buoys, set out in rows for the summer sailors, bobbed about like discarded party balloons.

After Easter, slender racing yachts with aluminium masts would begin to appear, like migratory birds. By June, the harbour would be crowded with boats of every shape and size, from small sailing dinghies to sleek, fat launches, their chrome and glass superstructure bristling with radar and radio antennae.

Sapphire-blue where the sun touched it, the restless water looked grey and very cold in the shadows of warehouses and shop-backs.

Shelley sucked in a lungful of salt-laden air and smiled. From the moment she had arrived three years ago, alone and desperate, the little Cornish town had proved the haven she so badly needed. Here, free from the unhappiness that had clouded her existence for so long, she had rebuilt her life.

The bell above the door tinkled as Shelley entered the little vegetarian take-away. The scent of fresh, crusty bread and savoury pies cooking made her mouth water.

'Hi, Janet,' she called. 'I'm back.'

Janet Penrose, a short, plump woman in her mid-thirties, bustled through the curtain of multi-coloured plastic strips that divided shop from kitchen, wiping her hands on a tea-towel. The front of her blue and white striped apron was dusty with flour and a lock of hennaed hair had escaped from the bright cotton scarf knotted at the back of her head.

'Did you have a good time?' she demanded eagerly. Her smile was warm and her eyes bright with interest.

Shelley sighed happily. 'Fantastic! I just lay by the pool in the sun and baked. Actually, that's not strictly true. I did go into the souk a couple of times. I saw some beautiful silver filigree, and I treated myself to a gorgeous caftan. I even rode into the Sahara on a camel to watch the sunrise.'

Janet shook her head. 'You've got more nerve than me, going to these here foreign countries all by yourself. Weren't you scared?' She lowered her voice. 'I've heard stories about Arab men, and the things you read in the papers—well!'

Shelley grinned. 'I must have been in the wrong place. Nothing remotely frightening happened to me. Anyway, Tunisia isn't exactly the back of beyond any more. It's very popular with tourists, especially Europeans seeking some sun.'

'You certainly look 'andsome,' Janet allowed. 'Brown as a nut you are. Your cough better, is it?'

Shelley nodded. 'It's completely gone.'

'That was some nasty dose of 'flu you had,' Janet commiserated.

Shelley dug into her shopping basket for her purse. 'I should think half the town has been down with it. Last summer was so wet I don't think we got the chance to build up any resistance.' She surveyed the display of home-made flans, pasties and pies, and the bowls of different salads behind the glass counter.

Janet pursed her lips. 'My Eddy says it's getting so we only have two seasons, June and winter. 'Twas dreadful for the visitors last year. Now, what are you going to have?'

'A mushroom quiche, a tub of winter salad with beansprouts and one of coleslaw,' Shelley decided and felt her stomach rumble.

'When did you get in?' Janet spooned diced vegetables, glossy with oil and vinegar dressing, from a large earthenware bowl into a shallow polystyrene tray and snapped the lid shut.

Shelley glanced at the thin gold watch on her brown wrist. 'Almost an hour ago. The train was only ten minutes late. It poured all the way down to Plymouth. But once we crossed the Tamar bridge, the sun came out.'

Janet shot her a shrewd glance. 'Anyone would think you were glad to be home,' she teased.

'Oh, I am,' Shelley acknowledged at once. 'The holiday has done me good but I love this place. It's the first *real* home I've ever had. I'll *never* leave here,' she murmured with quiet determination. Then, realising she had let her guard down, and aware of Janet's quick curiosity, she smiled brightly. 'I just dumped my case and came straight out. After five hours on the train I needed some fresh air!'

'I should think you get all the fresh air a body can stand, living down on the quay,' Janet's tone was dry. 'It's a wonder to me you haven't been washed away.

There's gales forecast again for next week.'

'Those cottages have withstood nearly a hundred years of Cornish weather,' Shelley retorted. 'They were built to last.'

'Oh, yes?' Janet was sceptical. 'How come Percy Bishop moved up to the old folks' bungalows, then? He always said they'd have to carry him out feet first.'

'It was his arthritis, not the cottage,' Shelley replied. 'He couldn't get up the slip and after Edna died last year there wasn't anyone to look after him. I think he was lonely. Anyway, I've still got Elsie on one side and Doreen and Frank on the other, and none of us intends to budge.'

Janet pulled a wry face. 'How many times have you had to sandbag the front doors this winter?'

'Only once, and that wouldn't have been necessary if the gale hadn't come at the same time as the spring tides.' Shelley smiled again, acknowledging her defensiveness over the little cottage. The strength of her protective feelings for the tiny two-up, two-down house with its two-foot-thick walls and small, square sash windows surprised even her on occasions.

Though Great-Uncle Nicholas had refused to sell it to her, he had promised she was safe there for as long as she wanted—at a fair and reasonable rent, of course. Shelley smiled inwardly. Virtually a recluse, communicating with her only rarely and then by letter, Great-Uncle Nicholas was, nevertheless, a true Trelawney. Business before everything. Hadn't Adam been exactly the same?

Adam. Shelley felt a gnawing hollow in the pit of her stomach. She looked down quickly, pretending there was something in her shoe. That was all in the past. Time healed all wounds and she had come a long way in three years. It wasn't the unexpected memory of Adam that was causing an aching tension in her muscles, it was the result of two days' travelling. As for the sensation of emptiness within her, it was nothing more than simple hunger.

Janet slid a golden-topped quiche carefully into a greaseproof bag and laid it on the counter top. 'You all right, my bird?' Her round face, flushed from the heat of the kitchen, mirrored concern.

Shelley forced a smile. 'Of course. Just a bit tired. The change of climate tends to come as a bit of a shock, too. That looks delicious.' She opened her purse. 'Honestly, Jan, I'm eating like a horse. My appetite has gone mad.'

'Good thing too,' the older woman replied. 'There isn't much of you at the best of times.'

Shelley's brown-gold hair, streaked by the hot north-African sun, fell forward over her shoulders as she surveyed her slender figure. Her faded denims were tucked into low-heeled ankle boots and a coral padded jacket covered a navy guernsey and beige and coral checked shirt. 'I don't know,' she frowned. 'If I go on eating at this rate, by the time summer comes I'll look like one of the little fat fishermen John Denny's always painting.'

Janet took the money and rang it into the till. 'Talking of John, I don't suppose you've been up to the Gallery yet.' Her tone made the words a statement and something in her voice brought Shelley's head up.

'No, I haven't.'

Janet picked up the tea-towel and absently wiped her hands again. 'Best thing,' she comforted. 'Tomorrow will be soon enough. After all, you only just got back. Best to have a good meal and a night's sleep before you face that lot.'

Shelley's forehead puckered in bewilderment. 'What are you talking about?'

'Bedlam up there it is.' Janet's Cornish accent grew stronger with her agitation. 'John and Sue Denny say you must have known all along. Gary won't have it, he says you'd never have gone off on holiday if you'd known. Kath isn't saying much at all, she's just looking worried. According to John, Gary isn't facing facts and is blind to the truth because he fancies you. Going at it hammer and tongs in here yesterday they were.'

Apprehension clenched icy fingers around Shelley's heart. 'Janet, *I don't know what you're talking about.* What about the Gallery? What's happened?'

Janet stared at her, then moved her ample shoulders awkwardly. 'It's been sold. There's a great notice up on the wall——'

'*Sold?*' Shelley gasped. 'It *can't* have been. There's some mistake.'

'Don't look like it, not by the size of that there notice.' Janet's tone was dry, but her eyes were full of sympathy. 'Here, don't forget your tea.' She pushed the two trays and paper bag across the counter.

'Thanks,' Shelley muttered, scooping them into her basket on top of the other groceries, and hurrying to the door.

'Now don't you go rushing up there and getting all upset,' Janet warned. 'You might have a suntan and a good appetite, but you was very ill. Let it wait till morning. A few more hours won't make no difference.'

Touched by her concern, Shelley flashed her a grateful smile, but her mind was made up. 'Jan, the Gallery is—was—rented in *my* name. If someone told you this place had been sold without your knowledge, would *you* leave it till another day to find out what was going on?'

Janet pulled a wry face, then frowned. 'Surely you should have had some notice? You paid your rent regular, didn't you?' When Shelley nodded, she went on, 'Well, then, isn't there some law——?'

'That's one of the things I intend to find out,' Shelley interrupted tremulously and pulled open the door. Above her head the bell tinkled wildly.

Janet called after her, 'Let me know——' but Shelley was already on her way up the street.

Her mouth was dry and her heart pounded painfully as her nervous system reacted to the shock. *There had to be some mistake.*

Great-Uncle Nicholas had rented her the old sail loft at the same time as the cottage. It was one of several properties he owned in the town and had been exactly what she was looking for.

She had instinctively known that people would be more interested in buying the delicate glass sculptures she created if they could actually see them being made. So she had set up her work-bench beside the largest window facing the street and, at right angles to it, several shelves and lighted cabinets displaying examples of her varied designs.

It hadn't taken long for the word to spread, though among the locals curiosity had outweighed sales. While pleasant and polite, Shelley made no effort to ingratiate herself. She wanted so much to belong, to make friends and become part of the community. But in closing the door on her past, she had also cut herself off from the usual talk of family and background by which the locals would weigh her worth and credibility. Guarding her tongue and her privacy, Shelley let her work speak for itself.

After she had inadvertently let slip to Janet at the take-away that her mother's maiden name was Trelawney, there had been a distinct warming of attitudes as this information sped along the grapevine. She volunteered no further information nor was any sought, but it was clear that being related to such an old and respected Cornish surname meant she was no longer an outsider.

A visit to a craft exhibition at the County Agricultural Show had really set the Gallery project on its feet. Overhearing a small group of exhibitors bewailing lack of workspace and the cost of leasing a shop in which to display and sell their work, Shelley had screwed up her courage and invited four of them to join her. She continued to pay the rent while they divided the other expenses.

John had painted and hung the sign after a conference had agreed the name and that first weekend they had worked late into the night to scrub, paint and construct partitions dividing the work areas and displays.

After Easter the early visitors had begun to arrive and by Whitsun the Gallery had been featured in the local press and on Duchy radio. It had been a difficult time for Shelley. While the others revelled in media attention, she was torn. She recognised the value of publicity for their work and was grateful for the orders and commissions that poured in. But behind her bright smile lay cold, writhing fear.

She tried to ignore it, to banish it with logic. She had altered her name and grown her hair long. Whenever photographers hovered, she loosened the finely plaited leather thong Gary had made for her, and let the thick, wavy tresses fall forward to hide her face. She tried to reassure herself with the knowledge that today's news was tomorrow's fish-and-chip wrapping, and that Great-Uncle Nicholas had promised not to reveal her whereabouts to *anyone* in the family.

An image of her parents that last evening sprang into her mind. Her father, tall, balding and distinguished in his dinner-jacket. Her mother, blonde hair elegantly upswept, wearing a long-sleeved sequinned black dress. A perfect foil for the diamond necklace sparkling on her still-youthful bosom. They had been on their way to an Embassy party. Three years ago. She had not seen them since.

Immersed in her thoughts, her gaze on the narrow pavement, she collided with someone coming down the hill. A hand caught her shoulder and she jerked backwards, her head snapping up.

'Shelley! How lovely! When did you get back? We

weren't expecting to see you till tomorrow.'

'Oh, *Gary!*' Shelley seized his hand, its calloused warmth immediately comforting as his fingers closed over hers. 'What's this about the Gallery being sold? Janet just told me. Gary, it *can't* have been. There must be some mistake.'

'I don't think so,' he said gently. Flinging an arm around her shoulders he drew her close. 'I've missed you. It seems ages since you went. Are you all better now? You certainly look . . . ' he made a soft whistling sound.

His milk-chocolate eyes were full of admiration. His brown hair was tousled as usual. Wearing a navy anorak over fawn cords, desert boots and a thick rust-coloured sweater, he was the same height as herself. Shelley felt a rush of affection for him. According to Janet, Gary had been the only one to defend her against rumour and suspicion.

'I'm fine,' she responded. 'But apparently I've been away too long.' She tried to smile, without success. Biting the inside of her lip, she met his gaze. 'I don't know anything about this.'

'For heaven's sake,' his eyes rolled impatiently, 'I never imagined you did.' He squeezed her shoulder reassuringly. 'It's not in your nature to be secretive.'

Shelley felt tension knot her stomach once more. *Oh Gary, if only you knew.* But about this he was right. Since the five of them had joined forces, all matters concerning the Gallery had been dealt with democratically, with each having his or her say before any decision was made. It had been Shelley's suggestion, even though, as official tenant, she need not have considered anyone's wishes but her own. So how *could* they have thought she would——

'Are you all right, Shell?' Gary was clearly concerned.

'What? Oh, yes. A bit tired, and this has been—well, rather a shock.'

'Come on.' He reached for her basket. 'I'll take you home.'

'No,' she shook her head decisively. 'I'm not going home until I've seen the others.'

'What for?'

'To explain, of course. Look, I'm perfectly all right. Honestly, I can manage. I expect you've got things to do.'

'Nothing that can't wait,' he grinned. 'Besides, that smells like one of Janet's quiches in your basket. As soon as you've said hello to John, Sue and Kath, I'll nip over to the off-licence and get a nice bottle of wine, and help you eat it. You can tell me all about your holiday.'

Shelley's heart lightened. It *was* good to be home. Gary's loyal friendship was balm to her strained nerves. 'And what about the meal your mother will be cooking at this very moment?'

'I'll have it for supper,' came the prompt reply, 'if my brother and sister don't get there first. You know Mum won't mind.' He paused. 'She's very fond of you.'

'Gary, she doesn't know me, we've only met a couple of times,' Shelley protested.

'That was enough. She says you've got *class*,' he teased.

Shelley swallowed, hiding her instant wariness with a quick smile. But it faltered as her thoughts returned to this latest and biggest problem. 'Who put the notice up, Gary? And when? Has anyone been in to see you about it?'

He shrugged. 'We don't know who put it up. It was there when John arrived to open the Gallery on Monday morning. He did mention some chap asking for you, but he thought it was a customer. Anyway, that was at the end of last week. Surely you've had a letter or something from an agent or solicitor?'

Her hand flew to her mouth. She thought of the

envelopes littering her doormat. 'Gary, I didn't even look at my mail. There's a pile of letters sitting on the table. Oh God, it must be in among those.'

'Don't fret about it, Shell,' he tried to comfort her. 'You weren't to know.'

'Yes, but if only I'd *looked*——'

'It wouldn't have made any difference,' he pointed out sensibly. 'OK, so you'd have learned about it in private rather than in public, but that wouldn't have *changed* anything.' He took the basket from her nerveless fingers and, drawing her arm through his, started back up the hill.

'The notice has caused quite a bit of speculation,' he said. 'But as no one has yet turned up to change the locks or throw us out, we've tried to carry on business as usual. Things are a bit edgy though,' he admitted.

'I'm not surprised,' Shelley was sombre. 'John is volatile enough on his good days. This lot must have sent him into orbit. How is Sue coping?'

'Pretty well,' Gary's grin was wry. 'She ignores him when he shouts, and refuses to argue. She and Kath have been going through the property pages in the local press. She sent John and I out to every estate agent in town to try and find other premises. But it's not going to be easy.'

'Gary, what would anyone want it for?' Shelley frowned in puzzlement. 'Eddy Trewin and some of the other fishermen use the bottom half for storing their nets and other gear, and their only entrance is off the wharf. We have the top half and our only entrance is from the street. I mean it couldn't be used for anything other than storage, the roof timbers are too low.'

Gary looked uncomfortable. 'The latest rumour is that the whole building is to be knocked down and holiday flats built on the site.'

Shelley felt the blood drain from her face. Suddenly cold, she shivered violently. 'What?' Her hair tumbled wildly over her shoulders as she jerked her head round. 'They can't!' she cried, 'They *can't*. Who is it, Gary?'

'I've never heard of them,' he shook his head, 'though the board has a local phone number on it.'

'But what's the name?' Shelley demanded.

'See for yourself.' Gary led her past the chandlery shop whose frontage hid the Gallery's entrance and front wall, which was set back several feet.

Attached to the left of the double doors, the notice-board was almost three feet square and painted orange, green and black. Shelley's lips quivered as she read, 'This property has been acquired for development by Trelawney Holdings.'

'Shell? Shelley? Are you all right?' Gary shook her lightly. 'You're as white as a sheet.'

'I'm—OK.' Her voice was hoarse and strained. She stared at the board. It couldn't be. Not down *here*. Fate couldn't be so cruel. She struggled to pull herself together. She was being ridiculous. There must be hundreds—thousands—of Trelawneys. She was tired and hungry. It had been shock enough to learn the building had been sold; seeing that name in these circumstances had thrown her off-balance.

With enormous effort, she stretched her mouth into a smile. 'Sorry, Gary. I hadn't wanted to believe—actually *seeing* the notice——'

'I understand.' He pressed her hand. 'Are you sure you want to go in now? It'll keep till the morning. It's almost five now.'

Shelley's heart began to pound. Her mouth was suddenly dry and the hair on the back of her neck prickled in age-old warning. She wanted to run. Clenching her teeth so hard that they ached, she made a brief movement with her head. She didn't trust herself to speak.

She started forward. Through the window she could see her work-bench. It was just as she had left it. Pots and jars containing the strips and rods of coloured glass with which she made her sculptures stood against the protective glass screen that edged her bench. Beneath the gas and air lamp set in a bracket just in front of her seat lay fragments of discarded glass, a blackened clothes-peg and her large tweezers.

The familiar sight was soothing and her panic eased. Gary released her arm and walked ahead through the hooked-back double doors. He opened the glass inner door and stood aside to let Shelley pass. Realising there were no customers he called, 'Hey, you lot, Shelley's home! It's been even more of a shock to her than it was to us, so go easy.'

The rhythmic whirr and click of Kath's spinning-wheel slowed and stopped as she pushed back her chair and came out to greet Shelley.

Sue was rearranging several vases of her flowers, perfect replicas of exotic blooms made in glorious silks and pastel chiffons. She looked round, a welcoming smile on her face.

Her husband glanced up from the picture he was framing, scepticism sharpening his tense, aquiline features.

Everyone started talking at once.

'I'm so sorry I wasn't here when all this blew up,' Shelley began.

Kath shrugged. 'If you didn't know it was going to happen, you couldn't have stopped it, anyway.'

'That's not important any more,' Sue cut in. 'Poor Shelley, what a welcome home.'

John erupted. 'For God's sake, Sue, what do you mean, it's not important? The tourist season starts in four weeks. But instead of selling our stuff and making some money, we'll be out on the street, with nowhere to work and no shop window!'

'Now lay off, John,' Gary warned.

'I didn't mean *that* wasn't important,' Sue tried to placate her husband.

The glass door slammed and they all swung round,

immediately silent.

His eyes glittered, hard as diamond, beneath the straight black brows, and his sensual mouth had a cruel twist. His voice matched his appearance, dark, cool, utterly confident.

'Good afternoon, Rochelle.'

There was a roaring in her head. *No!*

'Adam?' she whispered.

CHAPTER TWO

'WH-WHAT are you doing here?' He seemed taller than she remembered, and leaner, though the breadth of his shoulders beneath the charcoal suit clearly owed nothing to padding.

He slanted one black brow. 'I should have thought that was obvious.'

Shelley swallowed. 'That notice—Trelawney Holdings——'

'Is my company.'

'*Why*, Adam?' This latest shock had sent Shelley reeling, mentally putting her back to the wall. But now it was time to come out fighting. Anger flooded through her in a torrent, tearing at wire-taut nerves. 'Why *this* place? Is it some sort of revenge?'

Though his mouth retained a faint smile, his eyes were as cold and hard as steel. 'Rochelle, the purpose of my visit is to examine property which I now own. Why should you imagine there is anything personal involved?'

Acutely aware of the goggle-eyed and highly attentive audience, Shelley bit her lip, colouring painfully, and turned away.

'Look, just what is going on?' John demanded belligerently. 'Why do you keep calling her Rochelle?'

'It's her name,' Adam replied. 'Rochelle Barrington-Smythe.'

'Oh, really? We were under the impression she was called Shelley, Shelley Smith. At least, that's what she told *us*.' He glared at the others. 'Didn't I warn you? You lot might be gullible enough to believe she didn't

23

know what was in the wind, but not me. I had my
suspicions when that surveyor, or whatever he was,
came to inspect the building a month ago.'

'Come on, John,' Gary remonstrated, 'every building
on this side of the street was inspected. It was all to
do with the planned waterfront promenade.'

'So *he* said,' John said darkly. 'But it's plain as day
that these two know each other, and pretty well too,
by the sound of things.'

'Mr Denny,' Adam's voice was glacial, 'Rochelle
did not know about the Gallery's change of ownership. She couldn't have done. The situation arose
unexpectedly while she was abroad on holiday.'

'You seriously expect us to swallow that?' John
sneered.

Adam gave him the kind of look usually reserved
for something unpleasant on the pavement. 'Your
opinions are of no interest to me at all. However,' his
tone dripped sarcasm, 'I'm sure Rochelle must be
greatly comforted by your loyalty and support.'

John's eyes slid away and a dull flush spread across
his prominent cheekbones.

Kath cleared her throat. 'Mr Trelawney, when do
you want us to move out?'

'You have two weeks.'

'Two weeks?' John exploded. 'For God's sake, how
are we expected to find somewhere else in that time?'

'That's your problem,' Adam replied coldly. 'I
suggest you stop whining, and get out there and start
looking.'

'Do you think we haven't already been doing that?'
Sue sprang to her husband's defence. 'Being a stranger
here, Mr Trelawney, you may not be aware how hard
it is to find suitable premises. The high prices demanded
by landlords in summer make it even more difficult.'

'But you've had three years in which to save,' Adam
returned smoothly. 'During which time your expenses
have been minimal. Long enough, I would have

thought, to put something aside against such an eventuality as this.' His eyes glittered. 'Or did you intend to simply continue living off Rochelle indefinitely?'

'Adam, stop that at once!' Shelley spluttered. 'You have no right to say such things. These people are my friends.'

Adam's mocking gaze swept over each of them in turn before returning to Shelley, his brows arching in silent cynicism.

Gary pushed his hands into the pockets of his anorak. 'You seem to know an awful lot about us and our arrangements with Shelley,' he observed quietly.

Adam's narrowed gaze was speculative. 'And you would like to know where I got my information. Gary, isn't it? You work in leather. You bought a parcel of hides which had been retrieved undamaged from the wreck of a Spanish galleon, and along with your belts, wallets and briefcases, you sell a little bit of history. Smart thinking.' Adam nodded his approval. 'Your craftsmanship is of a high standard, too.'

Gary was clearly shaken. 'I've never seen you in here, so how——?'

Adam laid his index finger alongside his nose. 'I made it my business to find out. If you will all excuse us, Rochelle and I have several matters to discuss.'

'I bet,' John muttered sourly as Adam turned to open the door.

Shelley found her tongue. 'I'm sorry, Adam,' she announced defiantly, 'tonight is not convenient.'

He turned back slowly, his expression one of polite interest. 'Oh, really? Why not?'

'Because—because——' she went to Gary's side, picking up her basket from the corner of John's table, 'I've already made plans.'

His friendly smile didn't waver. 'What plans?'

'Gary is coming to my house for a meal,' she blurted.

Adam's smile faded as he shook his head. 'Don't encourage him, Rochelle,' he said pityingly, 'you and I both know you'll only let him down.'

Shelley caught her breath as the shaft, unexpected and so skilfully delivered, hit home, releasing a flood of pain-filled memories.

Gary shuffled his feet, visibly perplexed and uneasy at the tension vibrating between Shelley and Adam. 'Maybe we'd better leave it tonight, Shell.' He glanced sideways at her.

'No, Gary——' she pleaded, but he didn't let her finish.

'I'm not crying off,' he tried to grin, 'we've got some catching up to do. But I think tonight—well, it's pretty obvious you and Mr Trelawney have unfinished business to settle.' As Shelley shook her head violently and opened her mouth to protest, he added, with gentle emphasis, 'Concerning the Gallery.'

Shelley searched his boyish face with mounting desperation. It had all happened too quickly. She had not had time to work out all the implications. She only knew that Adam's reappearance in her life had shaken her far more deeply than she expected. She needed a breathing space, couldn't Adam see that?

No, unyielding and obdurate as ever, his own wishes were all that mattered to Adam Trelawney. Long-ago pain stabbed anew. Hadn't it always been so?

Realising suddenly the direction her thoughts were taking, and her unconscious, almost automatic, slide into acquiescence and defensiveness, Shelley stiffened. *No!* She had come too far and paid too dearly in pain, loneliness and tears to slip back now. Alone and unaided, she had built a new life. No one, especially not Adam Trelawney, was going to destroy it.

As her determination blossomed, adrenalin poured into her veins, quickening her heartbeat, sharpening her reflexes, preparing her mind and body to fight or flee. She had had her fill of running.

'Of course, Gary, you're quite right.' Shelley smiled and touched his arm, seeking, as much as giving, reassurance. 'Would you ask your mother if I can come to you for a meal next week instead?'

Gary's surprise was quickly masked by a wide grin. 'Sure. That'll be great. She'll look forward to it. She was only saying this morning how long it's been since she's seen you.'

From the corner of her eye Shelley saw Adam shake his head, but he said nothing.

Shelley gave Gary her brightest smile. 'Right then, it's a date.' She turned to the others. 'I'm so sorry about all this. I'll go and see a solicitor in the morning. We may be able to——'

'You'll be wasting your time,' Adam said bluntly. 'You had no security of tenure.' He caught her arm, drawing her towards the door. 'Let's go, Rochelle.'

'Don't call me that!' She swung round on him, trying to get free from his vice-like grip.

'Why not?' he shrugged. 'It's your name.'

'Not any more,' Shelley flared. 'I left it behind, with a lot of other things I no longer wanted.' Her stomach clenched into a tight knot as Adam's eyes turned to stone.

'Out!' he said softly, and opening the door, thrust her through it.

On the pavement she tried once more to wrench free. 'Let me go,' she hissed.

'So you can run away again?' A thread of steel underlay the sardonic question.

'I'm not running anywhere.' Shelley boldly met his cynical gaze. 'I live here, I work here, and I'm not leaving.'

The razor-edged east wind gusted up the street, blowing her hair across her face. She shook it back and shivered, clenching her teeth to stop them chattering. There was no one about. Most of the shops were already closed. The few late customers had all gone home and would be sitting in front of their fires, eating a hot meal and watching the news on television. Shelley thought of her little cottage and longed to be there.

As if reading her thoughts, Adam spoke abruptly. 'I'll drive you home.'

'No, thank you,' was her immediate response.

'Rochelle,' his tone was crisp and impersonal, 'there are certain things you have to know, and as I am not leaving until you are fully aware of all that has happened, you have a choice. We can remain here until you freeze to death, we can go to a pub and risk curious eyes and flapping ears, or we can go back to your cottage. It's up to you.'

'How do you know about my cottage?' she demanded uneasily. 'Have you been asking questions about me?' Her eyes were bright with suspicion.

'It wasn't necessary,' he answered. 'Shall we go?'

Realising he wasn't going to elaborate, she shrugged, then followed him up the road. Her eyes widened as he unlocked the Daimler and held open the passenger door for her.

'You seem surprised.' His tone was dry.

'I would have thought an Aston Martin or Lamborghini was more your style,' she retorted.

He smiled. 'I have nothing to prove,' then shook his head, as he continued, 'Assumptions are so often wrong, sometimes even dangerous.' The throaty engine purred as they glided out of the car park.

Anxious to break the silence and establish her control of the situation, Shelley observed, 'You must be what the Americans term a yuppie. Young, upwardly-mobile professional,' she explained as he raised a questioning eyebrow. 'Well on your way to your first million.' She thought her voice contained just the right amount of disdain.

A flicker of amusement crossed his face. 'I've never liked labels,' he replied. 'In any case, I've already made it.'

Shelley darted a startled glance at his profile. He was not boasting, merely stating a fact. Swiftly, she turned back to stare out of the windscreen. 'You must be very proud,' her tone was biting, 'making your fortune from destroying historic buildings and people's livelihoods.'

His only reaction was a slight tightening of his hands on the steering wheel. 'Restoration, where practical, is always preferable to demolition.' His voice was without expression. 'In fact, my company won two awards last year from the English Heritage Trust. However, in many cases there is no alternative.' Turning down the slip, he drew the car smoothly to a halt outside Shelley's cottage.

'Are you going to leave it here?' She leaned forward to retrieve the basket from between her feet.

'Worried about what the neighbours might think?' he taunted.

'Hardly,' she snapped, trying to ignore the warmth in her cheeks, for that had indeed been the thought uppermost in her mind. Elsie, the widow next door, was a dear—generous and kind-hearted to a fault. She was also an incorrigible gossip, inveterately curious and had eyes like a hawk. 'It's not likely you'll be here again. My concern was for the car. There's an east wind blowing and the tide is rising. There'll be a lot of spray. But you please yourself. After all, if this one rusts out, you can afford a dozen more.' Sliding out of the luxurious saloon, she slammed the door hard.

Once inside the cottage, Shelley placed her basket on the side-table and scooped up the letters, sorting through them.

Evidently deciding to leave the car to face the twin hazards of nosy neighbours and salt spray, Adam followed her in, ducking his head beneath the wooden beam above the door. 'What are you doing?'

'What I should have done as soon as I arrived home,' Shelley replied. 'There's a letter here somewhere that will explain—yes, this must be it.' She extracted a long, white envelope and tossed the others back on the table.

To her astonishment, Adam lifted it deftly from her fingers. 'I can tell you everything that's in there.'

'How clever of you,' she snapped. 'I prefer to see for myself.' She held out her hand. 'Please give it back.'

'Of course, but wouldn't it be more sensible to light the fire first?'

As she reached for the letter, her mouth opening to protest, he went on, 'Rochelle, the Gallery is mine now. Nothing is going to alter that fact. You've had a long day and a rather shattering homecoming.' He set the letter down on the table, apart from the others. 'There's plenty of time for this. If you'll tell me where the firelighters and coal are, I'll get a fire going while you make a cup of tea.'

'Nothing's changed, has it?' Her smile was bitter. 'This is the first time I've seen you since—in three years,' she amended hastily, 'and you're still issuing orders.'

His mouth twisted. 'Please forgive me. Naturally, you must choose. Which would you prefer, to light the fire or make the tea?'

'Oh, you're impossible,' Shelley snapped. 'There are some old newspapers and dry sticks in a box under the stairs, and the coal is in the bunker outside the back door.'

Snatching up her basket she marched into the kitchen, slammed it on to the table, then filled the kettle and plugged it in.

Glancing at her watch, she saw it was after six. The sun had set below the hills behind the town, and dusk was fast approaching.

Shelley flicked on the light and drew the red and

white check curtains. She unpacked her basket and, taking cups and saucers from the pine dresser, set them on a tray. Then she filled the matching sugar bowl and milk jug. Lifting the quiche out of its bag on to a baking tray, she popped it into the oven and tipped the salads into a glass bowl. As she reached for the bread knife, Shelley paused, watching Adam carry the coal scuttle in from the yard.

She was cold, tired and uncomfortably empty. The shocks of the past hour had drained her. If she didn't eat something soon she would faint. But she couldn't possibly have a meal without offering him something. She didn't want to eat with him; it was bad enough that he was here in her house. Sharing food with him would be tacit acceptance of his right to invade her life once more.

Still carrying the knife, she went to the living-room doorway. He had switched on the alcove lamps on either side of the fireplace, and drawn the curtains. The crushed rose velvet and lamplight gave the room a cosy intimacy heightened by the sight of Adam in his immaculate suit kneeling on the rug to hold a match to the paper and sticks.

Shelley felt dizzy with confusion. She *hated* him—didn't she?

Adam tossed the spent match into the leaping flames and straightened up, tall and lithe. He turned towards the kitchen, saw Shelley, and the knife clenched in her hand, and stood quite still.

Something flared briefly in his eyes and was gone. He waited. The silence stretched, broken by the crackling flames and the slap of water on stone as waves broke against the quay. 'The kettle's boiling,' he said easily.

She felt slightly light-headed. Adam's eyes flickered to the knife and his expression was quizzical. Shelley followed his glance, coloured hotly and almost dropped it.

'You had me worried there for a moment,' he quipped. But it was sympathy, not fear, she read in his gaze.

Anger rose in her again. She didn't want his sympathy, she didn't want anything from him. She could stand on her own feet. The last three years had proved that. 'I can't imagine why,' she replied coolly.

'Most murders happen within the family,' he said.

'I've never had the slightest inclination to murder,' Shelley retorted.

His voice was soft. 'Oh, I have.'

Shelley felt hot, then cold. 'No one is worth sacrificing my life for.'

'My sentiments exactly,' he agreed. 'The kettle is still boiling.'

Shelley dived back into the kitchen and pressed the switch. She dropped the knife with a clatter. Her hand was shaking.

'I'd like to wash my hands, if I may,' he said from the doorway.

Shelley was about to tell him to use the sink, but stopped herself in time. 'The door facing you at the top of the stairs,' she said without turning round. With faultless manners and a politeness she could not deny, he was exploring her home, and there was no reasonable way she could stop him. Damn Adam Trelawney!

Rinsing the pot, she made the tea, then slid a plate under the grill to warm and finished putting the groceries away. She heard the water in the pipes, but his reappearance in the doorway made her start. *He moved like a cat*. She knew he had noticed, and though he made no comment, she was as angry as if he had.

'Something smells good,' he remarked.

'Mushroom quiche,' she acknowledged tightly. Suddenly she wanted him gone. He was stirring up memories like silt in a pond. Why was he being pleasant? He had been his familiar arrogant self at the

Gallery.

'Are you going to invite me to share it?'

'Why should I?'

'Because you're too hungry to wait much longer, and too considerate to eat alone in front of me,' he pointed out.

As if backing the truth of his statement, Shelley's stomach gave a loud rumble. Leaning over, Adam picked up the tray.

'By the fire, I think.' His action left Shelley with no choice but to take the quiche from the oven and transfer it to the warm plate, then load a second tray with plates, cutlery, crusty bread, butter, tomato chutney and salad.

Adam replaced his cup and saucer on the coffee table and leaned back in the armchair. He looked utterly relaxed with his long legs stretched out, ankles crossed. 'That was delicious,' he pronounced. 'Where did you get the chutney?'

'I made it,' Shelley said matter-of-factly, stacking the plates and cups.

Adam looked surprised. 'I didn't know you went in for that sort of thing.'

'There's a lot about me you don't know,' she replied evenly, but her heart started to quicken. You never bothered to find out, did you, Adam Trelawney? It was sufficient that I was there, available when you had time for me, listening and admiring while you talked.

'I'm beginning to see that,' he acknowledged. 'You've changed, Rochelle.'

'Naturally.' She raised her eyes to his, her gaze cold. 'Three years is a long time. I've grown up, Adam.'

'I'm glad to hear it.' He was suddenly curt. 'Perhaps this new-found maturity will enable you to accept the inevitable, and persuade your *friends*,' he loaded the word with irony, 'that any ideas they may have about squatting or taking me to court are non-starters.'

'I'm quite sure such actions haven't even occurred to them,' Shelley said at once.

'Then you're more naïve than I thought,' Adam gibed. 'As for John Denny——' He shook his head in disgust. 'Why do you put up with his rudeness and tantrums?'

'You don't know John,' Shelley began.

'A point in my favour, I think.'

'He's a very talented artist,' Shelley went on, ignoring Adam's remark. 'But he's also rather highly strung. He had a breakdown about five years ago and tends to lash out when he feels threatened. It isn't personal. He'll be terribly apologetic when I go in tomorrow.'

Adam regarded her steadily from slightly hooded eyes. 'I wouldn't count on that.'

'Oh? What would you know about it?'

'Haven't you learned anything about human nature in this past three years? John Denny thought he knew you. You've worked in the same place, probably chatted at lunchtimes, all gone to the pub for a drink now and then. Suddenly, he realises you've been keeping secrets. Even your name isn't really your own. You say he's highly strung. He'll take all this as a personal affront.'

'That's rubbish,' Shelley replied.

Adam shrugged. 'Just make it quite clear that the property is legally mine, to do with as I wish.'

'And you wish to tear it down, to demolish a little more of the town's history, and deprive five people of their place of work!' Shelley flung at him. 'Still, I suppose that's how millionaires get to be millionaires, by climbing on other people's backs.'

Adam abandoned his relaxed sprawl, sitting up in the chair. 'Be careful, Rochelle,' he warned.

'Or you'll what?' She leaned forward on the sofa, her arms folded. 'Tell me, how did you persuade Great-Uncle Nicholas to sell it to you? It couldn't have been just the money, he had more than enough of his own. Civic responsibility? How the town would benefit from another block of flats for the summer visitors? Not mentioning, of course, the benefit to Adam Trelawney!'

'Stop it, Rochelle,' he rapped out.

'Why? Surely the truth can't hurt? After all, it's business, isn't it? And business has always been the religion of the Trelawneys.' She broke off, and swallowed, trying to control her hurt and anger. 'I never thought—it never occurred to me that Great-Uncle Nicholas could do such a thing.' Her voice faltered. 'He said the Gallery was mine for as long as I wanted it.'

'Rochelle,' Adam spoke slowly and distinctly, 'I didn't buy the Gallery from Nicholas.'

'No?' Her disbelief was plain. 'I suppose he *gave* it to you.'

'In a manner of speaking,' Adam agreed. He leaned forward in the chair, his hands linked, elbows resting on his knees.

As he hesitated, searching for words, the apprehension that Shelley had felt earlier returned. She tensed, waiting.

'Nicholas died two days after you left on your holiday,' Adam said gently. 'The Gallery was part of his bequest to me.'

Shelley stared at him, stunned. 'Nicholas is *dead*? How——?'

'A heart attack. It was all over very quickly.'

'*Dead?*' she repeated almost inaudibly, and her eyes filled. She stumbled to her feet. 'Excuse me,' she muttered, and would have fled from the room, but Adam barred her way, proffering a crisp, white handkerchief, careful not to touch her.

She wiped her eyes, keeping them lowered. It was difficult to get the words past the choking lump in her throat. 'The funeral——?'

'Very quiet, at his own request. None of the family

attended, except me. I was down here anyway.'

Shelley looked up. He was a dark blur. 'Adam, I should have been there. H-he was so good to me. He helped when I needed it most. He was the only one who understood——' She struggled to contain the sobs that hurt her chest, twisting the handkerchief between her fingers.

Adam made a slight movement, then abruptly turned away, thrusting his hands into his trouser pockets as he stared into the leaping flames.

Suddenly, something he had said made her stiffen. 'Why, Adam?'

'What?' He glanced round, his forehead furrowed, his thoughts clearly elsewhere.

'Why were you down here?'

'A private matter. Nothing to do with Nicholas's property. Though I did go to see him.'

'What for?' The question was out before Shelley could stop it.

'He was my grandfather, for God's sake,' Adam was brusque. 'I loved him too.'

Shelley tried to reconcile her warring emotions. She had been deeply fond of her great-uncle, and had tried to show her gratitude for his help in renting her the Gallery and cottage by writing him a long letter every month when she sent the rent to his agent. She described the work she had done on the cottage, the colours and fabrics she had chosen and, knowing how it would amuse and please him, she listed the bargains she had found, the haggling, and the discounts she had won. She told him the latest news from the Gallery, and any snippets of gossip circulating in the town. He never replied, but the agent had told her her letters delighted the old man, who loved to hear all that was going on, though he had no interest in being part of it.

Why, then, had he left the Gallery to Adam, who had no need of it? It wasn't that she wanted something for nothing. She would willingly have paid the estate a fair price. It would have meant a mortgage. But why hadn't he at least given her the chance?

And what about the cottages? 'Oh, no!' she gasped.

Adam glanced round, his expression darkening at what he saw on her face.

She had to moisten her lips before she could get the words out. 'Who—who got the cottages, Adam?'

He didn't reply, but the slight twist to his mouth was answer enough.

She screwed the handkerchief into a sodden ball and drew in a breath that wavered. 'That's it, then.' There was an aching tightness in her chest, and her throat was stiff. 'Congratulations, Adam. You've deprived me of both my home *and* my place of work. You must be really pleased with yourself.'

He swung round and the dishes rattled as his leg caught the corner of the low table. Her nerves raw, Shelley jumped. 'I didn't ask for them, Rochelle. I didn't buy them. They were thrust upon me.'

'Fine!' she flared back. 'So you're just an innocent victim of circumstances. Then sell the Gallery and this cottage to me.'

'No.' It was flat and final. 'You may stay here in the cottage for as long as you wish. The same applies to your neighbours.'

'How generous of you!' Her lip curled.

He went on as if she had not spoken. 'But you must be out of the Gallery in two weeks. Anything left inside when the contractors move in will be demolished along with the building.'

'Are you enjoying your power, Adam?' she asked with quiet bitterness. 'Does it make you feel good?'

He looked down at her, his eyes shadowed. 'Would you believe me if I said no?'

'Would you expect me to?' she retorted.

He shrugged and moved round the sofa to the front door. 'I suppose not. Thank you for the meal, I enjoyed it.'

Though she tried, Shelley failed to detect any irony in his tone.

'Goodnight, Rochelle. I'll be in touch.'

Shelley's chin rose. 'What for? Surely you've got everything now.'

His smile held genuine amusement, and she was suddenly sharply aware of his magnetic attraction. He was thirty-five years old and the past three years had not only pared any surplus pounds from his athletic frame, they had also imbued him with an aura of power. 'No, not quite.' His expression altered indefinably. 'However, I intend to remedy that.'

'I'll fight you, Adam,' Shelley threatened. 'I won't stand by and watch part of this town's heritage destroyed simply to put more money in your pocket.'

Throwing back his dark head, he laughed aloud, his teeth gleaming in the rosy lamplight. 'Normally I enjoy a challenge,' he chuckled, 'but I warn you, Rochelle, you're out of your depth in this one.'

'We'll see,' Shelley snapped grimly, trembling with anger at his arrogance.

The moment he was outside, she locked the door. His mocking laughter infuriated her. She would show him! She took a deep breath and deliberately relaxed her taut muscles. She was twenty-four, a successful, independent woman. Rage, no matter how justified, would solve nothing. Strength was what was needed. Strength, determination, and the money to hire a good lawyer to help her save the Gallery. The first two she had in abundance. The last posed something of a problem. While she made enough from her sculptures to live comfortably, she had not had time to save very much, ploughing all she earned into materials for her work and renovations to the cottage.

Shelley curled up on the sofa and stared in the fire. What should she do about the cottage? Pack and leave? Let Adam enjoy his ill-gotten gains? But where would she go? She could not afford to buy a new place, and a long let at this time of year would cost almost as much, even assuming she could find somewhere. Besides, Adam would say she was running away again. She could not, *would* not, let that happen.

In any case, she had invested too much of herself in the little house. She thought of the many months spent scraping and sanding, of the pounds of Polyfilla she had used, and the cramp in her arm from endless painting. There had also been the matter of the toilet in the backyard, until she had got council consent and Great-Uncle Nicholas's permission to convert the small back bedroom into a proper bathroom. She had turned the cottage into a comfortable, welcoming home, a secure retreat from the outside world. She would *not* leave.

She sighed deeply. If she stayed, she would be beholden to Adam. But how could she possibly waste precious time searching for another place to live? It would be hard enough finding somewhere to work. With her busiest time coming up, producing as many designs as possible, old favourites as well as new, experimental ideas, for the invasion of summer tourists, *she could not do it*. She had no choice. She *had* to stay.

CHAPTER THREE

SHELLEY cradled the steaming cup of coffee in both hands. Standing in the open doorway, she leaned against the frame and tilted her face up to the pale warmth of the morning sun.

Above the faint mist, wraiths of pink cloud streaked an aquamarine sky. The workboats, leaving their moorings, had all sails set to catch the gentle breeze that barely ruffled the water. The voices of the fishermen carried clearly, and Shelley couldn't help smiling at the succinct remarks bellowed from one boat to another and greeted with hoots of derision or roars of laughter.

Though warmly dressed in pine-green cords and an Arran sweater over a multi-coloured Viyella shirt, she shivered. She had slept badly, her dreams a vivid confusion of images. Voices had clamoured, past and present had merged and she had woken weary and emotionally exhausted.

All the problems yet to be solved began to close in on her. She shut them out of her mind and sipped her coffee. Just five minutes more, then she would go and face the others at the Gallery.

Taking another mouthful of coffee, feeling it warm her, Shelley let her gaze drift across the river to the small Georgian mansion which stood alone on the narrow peninsula.

If the house had a name, she had yet to learn it. The locals always referred to it as 'the house across the water'.

Backed by oaks and pines and set just below the

brow of the hill, its rolling lawns reached to the cliff edge. Below the cliff, which was not very high, wavelets lapped against jagged rocks.

Long, elegant windows were gilded by sunlight. In the neglected gardens, patches of yellow indicated clumps of daffodils forcing their delicate trumpets through a tangle of brambles, bracken and tall grass. From its toe-hold on the cliff-edge, gorse, with flowers like lemon butter beans, encroached on to the overgrown path.

Shelley looked at the house again, noticing for the first time the web of scaffolding encasing the flaking, once-white walls. The fine hairs on the back of her neck prickled with foreboding. Determinedly she shrugged it off. Change was a necessary part of life. She could hardly expect the world to stand still because familiarity made *her* feel more secure. It would be lovely to see the house and gardens restored. It was certainly an idyllic setting.

She finished her coffee, and turned the cup round and round in her fingers. Her reaction had been ridiculous, quite irrational. Yet understandable, surely? Hadn't she worked hard for three years, pouring all her energies into her work and home, carefully building herself a peaceful, protective cocoon in which to hide, only for much of it to be destroyed within the last twenty-four hours?

'Some 'andsome place, that is.' Elsie Penfold's broad Cornish accent interrupted Shelley's reverie. She straightened up and turned to smile at the little, white-haired woman, who had emerged from her own cottage to throw some crusts to the swooping gulls.

'I seen you come back last night.' Elsie's blue eyes were as bright and sharp as a bird's. 'Some fancy car that was. I never seen that down 'ere before. Friend of yours, is 'ee?'

Shelley had learned it was easier and safer to tell Elsie as much of the truth as was reasonable, for what she didn't know she would make up, and even that would be embellished when she passed it on at the Darby and Joan or the Women's Fellowship. Being a regular chapel-goer did not deter Elsie from listening to or passing on gossip. In fact, it often seemed to Shelley that the chapel provided the juiciest titbits. But, as Elsie said, 'If we was that 'oly, we wouldn' be there.'

Shelley forced a smile. 'No. He's the new owner of the Gallery.'

Elsie nodded, not in the least surprised. 'I 'spect 'e'll pull it down. Don't 'ave much choice really, do 'e?'

Shelley stared at her. 'What do you mean? Why not?'

'The foundations is cracking and there's dry rot in the roof. Tedn' safe no more.'

Shelley was stunned. 'Who——? How do you know? Are you sure?'

' 'Tis common knowledge, my bird,' Elsie shrugged.

'*I* didn't know,' Shelley cried. 'I pay the rent, but nobody bothered to tell *me,* or the others.'

'I s'pose everyone thought you knew.' Elsie tugged her old grey cardigan across her plump bosom.

'Where did you hear it, Elsie?'

'You remember Percy, from two doors along? Well, I see 'im at the Whist Drive last week. 'Is boy Ralph, you know, 'e married Margie Ferris's girl? They got three boys? 'Andsome lads they are, but that eldest one——'

'Elsie,' Shelley cut in, knowing if she didn't her question and Elsie's answer would be smothered and lost beneath a welter of irrelevant family detail. 'What about Percy?'

Elsie looked blank, then her wrinkled face cleared. 'Tedn' Percy, 'tis *Ralph*. 'E do work fer the council, up the planning office. 'E've been checking all the buildings along the waterfront because of that there new promenade. There's one or two more of they old places might 'ave to come down. Well, Ralph told Percy, and Percy was telling me. Dry rot, 'e said, and cracked foundations.' She cocked her head to one side. 'Coming again, is 'e? Your young man?'

'He's not my——' Shelley began at once, but Elsie appeared not to hear.

' 'E edn' short of a bob or two,' she observed shrewdly. ' 'Tis time you 'ad a man about the place. Girl your age do need a bit o' love. Tedn' natural you being all on your own.'

Hot colour flooded Shelley's face. Elsie had always believed in speaking her mind, but her remarks had never been *quite* so personal. 'I'm not lonely,' she defended. 'I've got lots of friends.'

'Tedn' *friends* I'm talking about.' Elsie was disparaging.

Shelley forced a smile to cover her confusion and the jolt Elsie's remarks had given her. 'Well, if he does come back, it will probably be to see you,' she said. 'He's your new landlord.'

Elsie gnarled hands flew to her mouth. 'Well, I never! I knew old Nick 'ad died, God rest 'is soul, but we wasn't told 'oo owned the property. 'Course we all 'ad letters from that there agent. 'E said as sitting tenants we was safe and didn't 'ave nothing to worry about. It do seem the new owner is 'appy with . . . existing arrangements.' Elsie frowned over the last two words. 'Do that mean the rent stays the same?'

Shelley nodded. 'I should think so.'

Elsie's face creased in a satisfied smile. 'Well, I think the next time 'e do come down, I'll 'ave 'im in for a cuppa tea.'

Shelley didn't stop to think. 'Don't you get any ideas about matchmaking, Elsie,' she warned. 'Even if Adam Trelawney was the last man on earth, I wouldn't——'

'It's that damp patch in my kitchen,' Elsie cut in

with an air of injured innocence. ' 'Tis making the
paper lift off the wall. It 'ave been worse since that
builder come in January.'

'Oh!' Shelley bit her lip, flushing scarlet, furious
with herself. She glanced at her watch. 'Lord, look at
the time! My first day back and I'm going to be late
if I don't run.'

'I 'eard there was 'ell to pay up there,' Elsie
announced with relish. 'Where you all going to go?
Staying together, are you?'

Shelley sighed. 'We just don't know. It's a real
worry.'

'Something will turn up, my bird,' Elsie comforted.
'You'll see.'

Shelley thought at first it might simply have been
her imagination. She *was* keyed up, and Elsie's rapier-
sharp observations had made things even worse. But
as she hung up her coat in the back room where they
stored materials and made the coffee, she knew it
wasn't. They were too quiet. Everyone had said hello,
but there was none of the usual chat and banter. Sue
hadn't even switched on her Phil Collins tapes.

With a sinking sensation in her stomach, Shelley
tied her hair back into a loose ponytail. Her hands
felt damp and she rubbed them down the sides of her
trousers. Then, taking a deep breath, she walked out
into the work area.

Kath was at her spinning wheel, seemingly intent
on drawing the twisted yarn from the spindle. Sue sat
at her table cutting petals out of stiffened scarlet silk.
Covered from chest to knees by a grubby white apron,
Gary was sorting through a box of heavy, raw-silver
belt buckles.

Still working on the frame he had been making the
previous evening, John looked up as Shelley passed
him.

'Well?' The word exploded from his lips, making
her jump.

'Well, what?' She smiled uncertainly.

'Oh, come on,' he snorted. 'Don't you think we're entitled to an explanation?'

Sheila shrugged helplessly. 'John, what do you want me to say? I told you yesterday I knew nothing about——'

'I'm not talking about the Gallery,' he butted in impatiently. 'I mean you and Trelawney. What's going on between you?'

Shelley stared at him. 'Nothing,' she spluttered. 'There's absolutely nothing going on——'

'There was though, in the past, something, wasn't there?' he accused.

'*If* there was, and I'm not saying it's true, I really don't think it would be any of your business,' she said quietly.

'Oh, no? We're losing everything because of him, and it's none of our business?'

'Aren't you exaggerating a bit?' Shelley kept her tone light, trying to make allowances. She hated scenes, and didn't want to antagonise him further. But his belligerence hurt and angered her. She was also furious at being forced to defend Adam. 'No one is stopping you from painting, or any of us from doing our jobs. We can work at home if necessary. Our biggest problem is an outlet, a shop-window.'

'*You* may be able to work at home,' John shouted, deliberately whipping himself into a fury. 'But I can't possibly paint in our flat. The light's all wrong for a start, and there just isn't enough room.'

'I'm sorry,' Shelley spread her hands, flinching backwards, 'really I am, but——'

'Who are you, anyway?' he demanded. 'I thought we were all mates. Three years we've been together, sharing the hassles, and building this place up into a well known craft centre. Now, all of a sudden, it turns out we don't know you at all.'

Shelley recalled Adam's warning. The angry man

glowering at her had clearly not given any thought to
the reasons *why* she had found it necessary to change
her name. He was concerned only with his own feelings
and had taken her behaviour as a personal slight.

'John, I'm still the same person who scrubbed this
floor and put up partitions with you. I chip in with
coffee money and cream cakes and a bottle of wine
on my birthday. We are both—all of us—creative
artists. What difference does it make what I call
myself?'

'Well, if it makes so little difference, why didn't you
tell us the truth?' he demanded with his own brand of
logic.

'I had reasons, very good ones, but they were—are
—personal,' Shelley replied. She glanced round. The
others had given up all pretence of working. They
were watching her, and waiting. She was both angry
and sad. Nothing would ever be the same again. She
really hated Adam in that moment. He had engineered
this situation. He had done it quite deliberately and
left her to face the consequences alone. She sucked in
a shaky breath.

'My full name is Rochelle Louise Barrington-
Smythe,' she spoke softly but clearly. 'My father is Sir
Richard Barrington-Smythe.'

'The financier?' Kath spoke for the first time. 'I
thought yesterday that name rang a bell, but I just
couldn't place it.'

'My God,' John was visibly shocked, 'you must be
loaded!'

'No, I'm not,' Shelley denied fiercely. 'I live on what
I earn from my work. When I arrived here three years
ago, I had five hundred pounds of my own savings. I
have not received one penny from my family, nor do
I expect to.'

'Why not, for God's sake?' John pushed thin fingers
through his lank hair. 'We needn't be going through
any of this. Your father could have bought this place,

and the rest of the street, out of petty cash.'

Shelley clenched her fists. She would not be drawn into speaking of her family. 'It wasn't for sale.'

'So how come Adam Trelawney is the new owner?' John's supercilious tone and expression reminded Shelley of a prosecuting counsel cross-examining a reluctant witness. He was convinced he'd caught her out.

'He didn't buy it,' she repeated. 'The building belonged to his grandfather who died recently. The Gallery was left to Adam in his will.'

'Your mother was a Trelawney, wasn't she?' Sue sounded puzzled. 'I remember Janet telling me——'

'Yes,' Shelley acknowledged wearily, waiting for one of them to ask the obvious question. It came from Gary.

'Are you two—you and Adam Trelawney—related, then?'

Shelley sighed, then nodded. 'His grandfather and mine were brothers. I think that makes us second cousins, or something similar.'

'So, you'll be all right then,' John sneered. 'He won't see you out on the street, blood being thicker than water and all that. I suppose you fixed it up between you during your cosy little chat last night. Got somewhere else lined up, have you? Going on your own this time? You won't want to be bothered with us any more.'

'Stop it, John!' Shelley cried. 'Sue, you can't believe I'd make any kind of deal behind your backs?' She swung round to Kath. 'Have you forgotten? *I* set this place up. It was a dream come true for me. Something I had always wanted. Don't you think I'm as shattered by all this as you are?'

Sue lifted one shoulder, plainly uncomfortable. 'Let's face it, Shelley, at least you've got a wealthy family to cushion you. We've got nothing.'

'But I *haven't*,' Shelley insisted. 'I'm on my own,

just as you are.'

Sue made no reply, but her expression, as she looked away, was sceptical.

'Is there any way we can fight, Shell?' Gary asked.

Shelley shook her head. 'Not that I can see.'

'What about his plan to knock the building down? I mean, is he really going to or was it just another rumour?' Gary queried.

'He's really going to,' Shelley replied tiredly.

'Couldn't we object to the planners? Ask the Civic Society to intercede on our behalf?'

Shelley shook her head. 'I thought of that. But apparently that survey carried out a month ago revealed dry rot and cracks in the foundations.' She gave another helpless shrug. 'Adam says repairs are not economically viable.'

'Adam says,' John mocked. 'And you're prepared to take his word?'

Shelley lost her temper. 'All right, what do *you* suggest we do? Have *you* got the money for an independent survey? Could *you* afford to pay for the repairs? Are *you* going to finance the court case it would take to get this building designated of historical and architectural interest—assuming, of course, that it actually *is*? And having done all that, you still have one more problem to deal with. *The property belongs to Adam Trelawney.*'

Gary went swiftly to her side and put his arm around her shoulders. 'OK, Shell, it's all right, no one's blaming you.' He glared at John.

'Really?' She gulped back tears. 'I thought that was exactly what you were all doing.'

'No need to get upset, Shelley,' John muttered awkwardly.

'Oh, isn't there?' she flashed back. 'You accuse me of lying, deceiving you and making deals with a man I wouldn't even give a cold to, but I mustn't get upset. You use *me* as a verbal punch-bag on which to vent

all *your* worry and frustration, but *I* mustn't get upset.
Maybe you were able to choose your grandparents, I
wasn't so lucky. But because I happen to be related
to Adam Trelawney *you* immediately see a conspiracy.
Yet *I* mustn't get upset. Well, for once he was right,
John. With a friend like you I'll never need enemies.'

In the ensuing shocked silence she pulled free of
Gary. Struggling to steady her breathing, her heart
pounding, she crossed to her work-bench and sat
down, her back to them, biting her lip to hold back
the tears. She felt betrayed and terribly alone. Right
though he may have been about John, this whole,
horrible scene had been Adam's fault. Through his
arrogance, his deliberate lack of explanation regarding
the true state of the building, and his insistence on
using her real name even though he must have known
she had altered it, he had deliberately contrived to
throw suspicion on her.

He said it was not revenge, but what other motive
could there be? It was obvious he was trying to drive
a wedge between her and the only people she could
call friends. Though she had to admit only Gary really
fitted that description. Why would he want to do that
if not for revenge?

Automatically, Shelley tested the gauges and valves
on the gas and oxygen cylinders. Both were over half-
full. Next, she checked the lamp in which they were
mixed, making sure it was firmly attached to the bench
in front of her, the nozzle pointing away at the correct
angle. She turned on the jet and lit it with a match,
adjusting the flow from yellow to blue-white to raise
the temperature.

She took a strip of grey, opalised glass resembling
mother-of-pearl from one of the jars on the far side
of the bench. Selecting a thin rod of clear glass from
the fragments littering the area in front of the lamp,
she moved the ends of both into the flame which flared
yellow as it licked around the glass.

Feeling her tension subside as her attention focused
on the glowing blob of melting glass forming on the
end of the strip, Shelley rolled it up with the rod. With
smooth, confident movements, she drew a thin rope
of shimmering glass away from the now elongated
blob, then deftly curved it back on itself, finishing
with a fine point. She flamed the rod and broke the
contact. Picking up a pair of flat-ended tweezers, she
gently shaped the protruding point, made indentations
for eyes, and suddenly the curved rope became the
head and neck of a heron.

Concentrating entirely on the sculpture, alternating
rod and tweezers to coax the rest of the bird from the
molten glass, Shelley was barely conscious of a shadow
outside the window.

When she had first started to work in public she
had found it terribly difficult to concentrate. Once
aware of an audience, her hands would begin to shake.
Many a distorted bird and flower had ended up among
the fragments.

But gradually she had schooled herself to blank out
everything but the glass and the flame. Now it was
automatic, and the rigid discipline had provided an
unexpected dividend. Not only had her talent
blossomed and her repertoire grown, but she had
achieved in the total concentration a peace of mind
she could not capture anywhere else, not even in the
cottage.

She finished the heron's legs, one drawn up and
bent at the knee, the other straight, its large foot
perfectly balanced so that the bird could stand, rock-
steady, without any other support, on the glass shelf
in the window.

As she placed it, Shelley realised the shadow had
disappeared. However, as she began to work on
another sculpture, a high-heeled slipper in transparent
glass, she was vaguely aware of its return. Another
shy customer, she concluded. There were plenty of

those. People who loved to watch, but were reluctant to come inside and buy. Though many did, after returning two or three times to hover and stare. Shelley gave a mental shrug and devoted herself to the slipper.

Gary brought her coffee over but, knowing better than to distract her, merely placed it near the edge of the bench and went quietly back to his own work.

The door opened and closed several times as browsers and customers came and went. Sue had switched on her tapes and the rhythmic music throbbed softly in the background, accompanied by the whirr of Kath's spinning wheel and the sound of Gary's heavy sewing machine.

Shelley placed the slipper next to the heron, and flicked off the jet. She leaned back, eyes closed, and yawned, raising her arms to stretch luxuriously.

When she opened them again to reach for her coffee, she found herself staring directly into the cool grey gaze of Adam Trelawney. She froze, immediately tense and wary.

'What do you want?' She kept her voice low, all too aware that, despite the apparently normal activity going on behind her, they were being watched.

'Such charm,' he murmured laconically. 'Do you greet all your customers like that?'

'You're not a customer,' she retorted.

'As a matter of fact, I am. I want to buy that,' he pointed. 'I watched you make it. A fascinating experience.'

So he had been the elusive shadow. Shelley's skin tingled, and she couldn't understand why. She was used to being watched while she worked. *But not by Adam.*

'It's amazing.' He shook his head, clearly intrigued.

'Actually, it's a heron,' she replied, straight-faced. 'And it's not for sale.' To disguise her nervousness she took a sip of her cold coffee, replacing the mug with a brief grimace.

'To anyone, or just to me?' Adam's eyes gleamed, but whether with anger or amusement Shelley could not tell.

She searched wildly for an excuse. Her reaction had been purely instinctive and, now she considered it, quite irrational. But she was finding it very hard to keep a cool head where Adam was concerned.

Using the awesome power of his personality, plus the irrefutable fact that the law was on his side, he was invading her life with all the tact and finesse of a conqueror, and she lacked both the confidence and experience to counter-attack.

She was astute enough to recognise that his actions and behaviour were part of an overall plan. But to what end? Whatever it was, she didn't want to know. She didn't want him in her home. She did not want him to buy her work. Like the sticky strands of a spider's web, every contact she had with him was drawing her into danger. Her own honesty forced her to admit that part of the peril lay in his magnetic attraction. An attraction on which she had deliberately turned her back, and yet had never quite managed to extinguish.

'I—I'm trying to build up my stock for the summer. I have to display as wide a range as possible and I'm several weeks behind.'

'Ah yes, your influenza.' He leaned forward slightly, studying her. 'You still look a little tired. Yesterday must have been something of an ordeal.'

'Oh, it was,' she murmured, averting her eyes. He would never know just how much.

'Let me take you out to dinner this evening,' he coaxed softly. 'I owe you for that delicious meal last night.'

'That's not necessary,' Shelley replied stiffly, wondering what the others were making of Adam's reappearance and the hushed conversation.

'Oh, but it is,' he insisted. 'It is a rule of mine always to repay hospitality.'

Shelley sensed waves of disapproval emanating from John. The unfairness of it hurt. With the exception of Gary they had all blamed her, and even he had backed off from argument or confrontation with Adam. Shelley sighed. She couldn't blame Gary; Adam had that effect on most people.

She raised her eyes. 'You don't owe me anything,' she said firmly.

'No, but *you* owe *me*,' came the instant reply.

Shelley's throat went dry. 'I don't know what you're talking about.'

His eyes glittered, ice-cold and diamond-hard. 'I think you do. But allow me to refresh your memory——'

'No!' she blurted, acutely aware of watching eyes, of ears straining to hear what was going on.

'We have to talk,' Adam's tone was determined.

'There's nothing to say.' Shelley could feel beads of sweat forming on her forehead and upper lip. She did not dare wipe them away. There was still a chance he might not have noticed.

'After three years?' he rasped, and she flinched at his bitterness. 'You demand choices, well, I'm offering you one now.' He rested one arm casually on top of the glass screen. 'Dinner tonight, or we talk here and now. Doubtless your friends would be as interested as I am to learn why you walked out on me two days before our wedding.'

Shelley stared at him. 'You wouldn't——' she choked.

'Try me.' His smile was cold and cruel. 'I'll pick you up at seven.' He turned and walked out without a backward glance.

How she got through the rest of the day, Shelley never knew. The others said little though their curiosity was all too plain. Gary wanted to take her for a drink at lunchtime but she declined. 'I'm lousy company today, Gary,' she apologised. 'I've rather a lot on my mind.'

'That's OK, Shell.' He smiled reassuringly. 'We'll make up for it next week.'

She nodded vaguely and turned away.

'You've forgotten already.'

She glanced at him, startled.

'The meal, at my place,' he reminded her. 'Mum's over the moon. She's started planning already.'

Shelley swallowed and tried to smile back. 'Of course I haven't forgotten,' she lied, 'I'm looking forward to it, Gary.' She touched his arm hesitantly, 'Don't let your mother go to too much trouble. I—well—it's only a meal.'

'Just try stopping her,' he grinned. 'Anyway, you're worth it.'

In an effort to escape her churning anxiety, Shelley threw herself into her work. By five o'clock she had completed two blue-grey dolphins, a ballerina in opalescent peach, and the first of a planned vaseful of green and white snowdrops. Her neck was stiff and her back ached, but her fear of the coming evening had faded, replaced by a nervous resolve.

As she lay soaking in the bath, she gave herself a pep-talk. Whether by accident or design, Adam had found her. But she was a very different person to the one who had left him three years previously. This was her chance to make him realise she had a life and a career of her own. She was a person in her own right, no longer simply one man's daughter and another man's fiancée.

She dressed with care, choosing a black velvet skirt and a cream silk blouse with full sleeves and a low-collared V-neck and bow. After brushing her hair until it shone, Shelley piled it into a loose chignon which left tendrils curling softly on her neck and temples. Mascara and rose lip-gloss were all the make-up she could handle, for her fingers, as they fastened the double strand of pearls around her throat, were cold and shaking.

This was ridiculous, she told herself. What was she nervous about? Adam Trelawney meant nothing to her. He was simply part of the past. And that could not touch her now.

Nevertheless, his knock, when it came at two minutes to seven, caused her heart to hammer painfully against her ribs.

Moistening her lips, she drew in a deep breath and opened the door, turning away almost at once. 'I'll fetch my coat. Please come in.'

'How kind.'

His irony, made her throat and face grow warm. But what did he expect?

'Do you have some water?' he enquired pleasantly.

Shelley paused on the third stair, her fingers curling into her palm. Was that a dig at her lack of hospitality, her hurry to get him out of the house again? She turned to look down at him. 'There's some dry sherry in the dresser, the right-hand cupboard.' Hardly a gracious invitation, but she wasn't feeling very gracious. Despite all her resolve, she was horribly nervous.

'I think water would be more suitable, don't you? He moved the hand half-hidden behind his back, revealing a cellophane-wrapped bouquet of multi-coloured carnations, tied with a large bow of pink ribbon.

Speechless, Shelley stared at the flowers, then at Adam.

'Water?' he prompted. As she started back down the stairs he waved her away. 'I'll see to it. You get your coat.'

'Th-there's a vase in the cupboard under the sink,' she stammered. He nodded and strode into the kitchen, and Shelley fled upstairs. He had her completely off-balance. She was under no illusion that good manners or consideration for her feelings would deter him from using any means within his power to get his own way. He had quite openly blackmailed her into having dinner with him. So why the flowers? Why pretend this evening was a special, looked-forward-to occasion? Perhaps it was. Maybe his Jekyll and Hyde approach was deliberate, part of some plan to avenge his wounded pride.

Shelley closed her eyes and pressed cold hands to her burning face. She was behaving like some cornered animal. She had nothing to fear. She had done nothing wrong. If she was guilty of anything it was that she had recognised the truth before it was too late, that marriage to Adam Trelawney would have destroyed her.

As she reached the bottom of the stairs there was another knock at the door. Adam, his suit jacket unbuttoned, hands in his trouser pockets, was standing on the rug with his back to the fire, totally at ease. Gazing at Shelley from hooded eyes, he raised one dark brow.

Tossing her classic fawn cashmere over the back of the sofa, Shelley opened the door and Elsie peered in.

'Some pretty sight you are,' she stared admiringly at Shelley. 'Going out, are you?' Then she spied Adam. 'Mr Trelawney, idn' it? I thought I 'eard your car.' Her eyes flicked to Shelley and back. 'You must 'ave a golden tongue, Mr Trelawney. Shelley was telling me jest this morning she wouldn'——'

'What do you want, Elsie?' Shelley cut in, her cheeks aflame. But Elsie would not be rushed.

'Going out somewhere nice, are 'ee? A celebration is it?'

'Just a meal,' Shelley held on to her patience. 'Was it important?'

'What?' Elsie dragged her sharp little eyes from Adam.

'What you came to see me about.'

'Oh, well, not really. I mean, I don't want to bother you.'

'What *is* it, Elsie?'

'A couple of eggs. I'm baking, see. Making buns for the cake stall up the Women's Institute tomorrow. I done a sponge and a slab of 'eavy cake, but I 'abn' got no more eggs.'

Shelley went towards the kitchen. 'Will two be enough? I've got an extra half-dozen if you want them.'

'No, two's all right.'

Shelley took the eggs from the fridge, put them into a spare carton and returned to the living-room.

'Can't promise tomorrow,' Adam was saying. 'Would Sunday be convenient?'

'That's 'andsome,' Elsie beamed. 'I don't like to make no fuss——'

'Don't worry about that, Mrs Penfold,' Adam soothed. 'As soon as I've seen what needs doing, I'll get someone on to it straight away.'

'Lovely you are.' Elsie's eyes danced. 'Right, I'm gone. Enjoy yerselves, now.' She bustled to the door.

'The eggs, Elsie?' Shelley reminded her.

'What?' The old woman looked bewildered.

Shelley held out the carton.

Elsie grinned and hugged it to her bosom. 'Ferget me 'ead if 'twadn' screwed on. See 'ee again.' She gave Shelley a huge wink and disappeared into the dusk.

CHAPTER FOUR

SHELLEY cradled the balloon glass in her palm, swirling it gently so that the ice-cubes tinkled and the Cointreau released its sweetly pungent aroma.

The meal, in the town's leading waterfront restaurant, had been delicious. Chilled melon and parma ham, followed by baked trout garnished with lemon and parsley, and served with mushrooms, shrimps, baby carrots and peas. And for dessert, a mouthwatering confection of meringue and strawberries topped with clotted cream. The dry white wine had been light and delicate, complementing the food perfectly, and Adam's behaviour as host could not have been faulted.

As they walked the short distance to the restaurant, he had spoken of Nicholas's affection for the town and his own observations of the changes taking place. Ready to criticise, she had instead been reluctantly impressed by his grasp of the problems facing both developers and conservationists.

The restaurant owner, a man renowned for his disparaging manner towards those he considered unworthy to grace his establishment, took one look at Adam and, with a subservience that surprised and amused Shelley, insisted upon attending them himself. Adam accepted the lavish attention as perfectly normal, and Shelley realised wryly that for him it was.

Against her will she found herself smiling, then laughing aloud at the stories he told, often against himself, concerning various properties he had bought and restored. He steered the conversation on to her own cottage and the improvements she had made, asking questions which, while in no way ingratiating, showed a keen interest in her choice of colours, fabrics and styles.

Just as she began to grow slightly restive, suspicious of his reasons, he switched with smooth ease to relating snippets of gossip concerning people she had known in London.

Despite her determination to remain aloof and on her guard, Shelley began to relax under his effortless charm. She tried to resist his droll humour and barbed wit, but her resolution soon melted and she found herself responding, shyly at first, then with increasing confidence.

She felt like a newly hatched butterfly emerging from its chrysalis, like a flower opening its petals to the sun after a long, hard winter. Sipping the crystal liquid which Adam had suggested as an alternative to brandy, Shelley found it refreshingly cool on her lips then warm on her tongue. She lowered the glass, gazing pensively into its depths.

It was so long since she had been taken out like this. She sometimes went with Gary to the pub for a drink, and occasionally they would pick up a Chinese take-away. But this—witty and wide-ranging conversation, delicious food, beautifully presented and expertly served against a background of crisp linen, sparkling silver and fresh flowers, with candle-light, soft music and a three-quarter moon casting a shimmering silver path on the restless black water beneath their window—how long was it since she had enjoyed such luxury?

Three years. It came to her with a shock. The last time—the last time had been with Adam, a week before the date set for their wedding.

Involuntarily, she glanced up. He was watching her, his eyes unreadable, his cruel, sensual mouth set in an imperceptible smile.

He knew what she was thinking as clearly as if she had spoken her thoughts aloud. *He had planned it*. Expertly guiding and controlling the conversation, he had anticipated her suspicions and doubts, and had smoothed them away before she was even aware of them forming. He had skilfully bypassed her defences, peeling them away like onion skins, and had forced her to recognise, despite her full and busy life, the core of emptiness at its centre.

Feeling exposed and painfully vulnerable, Shelley lowered her eyes quickly. She set the glass down with great care and, reaching for her evening bag, made to get up.

Adam's hand snaked across the table and covered hers. 'No, Rochelle, no more running,' His voice was low and throaty and his eyes bored into hers.

His touch sent an electric tingle along her arm, and heat flooded her face like a tide. She tried to snatch her hand away, terrified he would sense what was happening. But his fingers curled around hers, holding them fast. 'Please?' he added softly, the wry twist to his mouth an acknowledgement of what the word cost. Command came easily to him, but having to *ask* for something was a rare occurrence in Adam Trelawney's life.

Shelley kept perfectly still. Anything to make him let go. She moistened her lips. The moment had come. It was a measure of his charm, so potent when he chose to employ it, that she had briefly forgotten the reason for their being together that evening. Doubtless he had planned it that way, to force her off-balance. Suddenly, all the light went out of the evening. 'What do you want, Adam?' she said dully.

Seeing she was no longer poised to flee, he released her hand and, lifting his glass, swallowed deeply, his eyes never leaving hers. 'The truth,' he replied. 'Why did you do it, Rochelle? Why did you go like that, without a word?'

Shelley clasped her hands tightly together in her lap. 'It was a matter of survival,' she whispered. 'I had no choice. Besides, I left you a note.'

His face darkened. 'That told me precisely nothing.' He leaned forward. 'Survival? What the hell are you talking about? You had everything.'

Like a hunted animal, Shelley glanced round. The restaurant was filling up. Clinking glasses and the discreet clatter of cutlery were overlaid by the murmur of conversation and laughter. 'Could we leave now?' she pleaded. 'I—I'd like to have some fresh air.'

He studied her for a moment. 'As you wish.' He snapped his fingers. Instantly, the owner appeared at his elbow, making washing movements with his hands, anxious that everything had been to sir's satisfaction.

While Adam settled the bill, Shelley escaped to the ladies' room. She repaired her lipstick with trembling fingers, her eyes dark and haunted. He was stirring up old hurts, old memories, and there was no escape. She should have realised the moment she saw him that it would come to this. He had a right to know. Yet would he ever understand?

Their footsteps echoed as they walked through the quiet street. Shelley had belted her coat tightly and turned her collar up against the night chill. Adam, apparently impervious to the cold, left his sheepskin unbuttoned, his hands pushed deep into the pockets.

On leaving the restaurant, Shelley had deliberately turned left, away from her cottage. If they had to talk it was best done outside, on neutral territory.

As they forked left again, down the slope on to the quay in front of the Custom House, she tried desperately to impose some sort of order on her thoughts. A snatched glance at Adam's set face warned her that time was running out.

Fishing boats bobbed within the sheltering arms of the quay. A street lamp reflected rainbows on the oil-streaked water. But Shelley turned her back on the picturesque scene and, resting her forearms on the grey-painted railings, gazed out across the black expanse of the harbour.

Adam stared down at her, leaning on one elbow, so close that his coat brushed hers. 'Well?'

Shelley looked up but his face was in shadow and she could not read his expression. 'You're right,' she said softly, 'to an outsider it must have looked as though I had everything.'

'Poor little rich girl,' he mocked, then his tone changed. 'I was no outsider, Rochelle,' he grated. 'We were to be married.'

Her gaze slid away, focusing on the ruffled water. 'What's the point of all this, Adam?' she said wearily. 'It's not going to change anything.'

'I want an explanation, Rochelle, and neither of us is leaving here until I get one.' There was no anger or threat in his voice, just cold, inflexible determination.

'I——' She twisted her fingers, linking and separating them, unable to look at him. 'It wasn't just you. It started long before that. But you—the wedding——' Shelley cleared her throat, struggling to keep her voice level. 'You see, my parents couldn't accept that what they planned for me wasn't what *I* wanted. I had to fight to be allowed to go to art school. All my mother could see was way-out clothes, multi-coloured hair and drugs. It took me a long time to persuade her that none of those were compulsory. Then, when I finished my basic course and wanted to specialise, it meant studying glass-blowing techniques with a company making scientific instruments. Totally unsuitable, they said.' Shelley's sad smile had a bitter edge to it.

'My father even went to the trouble of finding out and warning me that of all the students all over the country who attempt the course, only two or three make the grade. He only wanted, so he said, to spare me the disappointment of failing.' Shelley's mouth twisted. 'It apparently didn't occur to him that I might succeed.' She was quiet for a moment.

'What did *they* want?' Adam prompted.

Shelley glanced sideways at him. 'For me to go to a finishing school in Switzerland and do a cordon bleu cookery course because it would be so useful when I married and gave dinner parties.'

'That doesn't sound so unreasonable,' Adam pointed out mildly. 'I know a few girls who'd have given their right arms for an opportunity like that.'

'No doubt,' Shelley gritted, 'but I knew what I wanted to do, and it didn't include spending hours slaving over a stove.'

'What has any of this to do with me, with us?' he demanded.

'Do you really need to ask?' Her retort was bitter. 'It was only when my grandmother and Great-Uncle Nicholas got together and threatened to remove their investments from father's control that he conceded defeat and I began working with glass. But though my father had lost that battle, he was still determined to win the war and return me to what he and my mother considered the proper way of life for a girl of my background and social standing. So the next thing he did was find me a fiancé. Don't deny it, Adam,' she flared as he made to speak.

He shrugged and remained silent, but she sensed, despite his casual stance, a new stillness.

'I know my father, he's very astute.' The muscles in Shelley's face felt stiff and she shivered, hot then cold, recoiling from the shame and hurt that her father could use her as a commodity to be bartered. Yet even worse, her own treacherous heart had played into his hands, for she had fallen in love with Adam Trelawney and her innocent body had quivered and sung at his lightest touch.

'You had all the necessary qualifications,' she said lightly. 'You were educated, charming, good-looking,

and ten years older than me.' Shelley's cheeks began
to burn and she was grateful for the darkness as she
stumbled on. 'You were obviously experienced with
women and my mother made it clear I should be
thankful, for if my wilfulness and naïveté bored you,
at least you would be discreet about your mistresses.'

She heard his sharp intake of breath, but dared not
stop. He had wanted the truth and he was getting it,
but she doubted she would ever find the courage to
repeat this ordeal.

'You were making a name for yourself, as well as a
great deal of money, in the property market. But what
really clinched it in father's eyes was that we were
already related, though not closely enough for it to be
a problem. It was the perfect match.' Shelley turned
her head away, glad of the cold night air on her hot
skin. Surely it shouldn't still hurt like this?'

'You seem to have forgotten something,' Adam said
softly, and her heart gave an unexpected and painful
kick. But as soon as he spoke she realised he was
giving nothing away. They were here only because he
wanted information. Why it mattered after all this
time she didn't know and could not guess. Pride,
perhaps? Or revenge? Adam had always kept his
innermost thoughts and feelings locked up, and she
had never found the key.

'I'm nobody's pawn,' he said. 'I did not seek or
need your father's patronage. I was attracting plenty
of recognition by my own achievement.'

'Oh, yes, you worked hard,' Shelley agreed. 'You
talked of little else.'

His voice was glacial. 'I assumed, foolishly it
appears, that you would be interested.'

Shelley swung round to face him, calmly meeting
his cold gaze. 'I was. But you didn't want discussion,
Adam. You weren't interested in my opinions. You
talked *at* me, not to me. I was merely a sounding
board.'

'*That's* why you ran away?' He was scathing. 'Because *you* were not always the centre of attention?'

Her eyes widened. 'Is that what you think?'

He raked one hand impatiently through his thick hair. 'What do you expect?'

They glared at one another. As the silence lengthened, the tension between them mounted.

'Nothing,' Shelley replied eventually, her voice carefully devoid of expression. 'Nothing at all. I'd like to go home now.' She had barely taken a step when Adam gripped her arm and pulled her round to face him.

'Explain!' he demanded.

Shelley tilted her chin. 'I had a job too, Adam, and ambition. The work was difficult. Every day brought new problems and I was plagued by doubts. I needed someone to listen, to encourage me. But you never had time. *Your* work was all that counted for you.' She could feel his fingers through her coat. She would have bruises tomorrow, but pride kept her silent.

'I was building our future,' he snarled. 'What *you* had was a hobby.'

'That says it all!' Shelley wrenched free, shaking with a sudden, violent surge of anger. '*That's* what I ran away from, selfishness and manipulation. First my parents, then you. All of you trying to mould me into what *you* thought I should be. My mother wanted a mini-version of herself, my father wanted an alliance to cement the family fortunes, and you—what role was I suppose to play for you, Adam?' She tossed her head in frustration and disgust. 'None of you cared what *I* wanted. I was simply an extension of *your* ideas.'

He put out a placating hand. 'Rochelle——'

'No,' she cried, backing away, '*you* listen for once. No one has the right to tell me how to live my life, or to be disappointed because I'm not what they expected or planned that I should be. My talent for glass sculpting may not rate very highly on your scale of importance, but I love what I do and I can earn enough to support myself.' She stopped, breathing fast, her heart racing. 'I don't need you, Adam Trelawney. I don't need anyone!'

'Congratulations,' he said tersely, his expression stone-hard. 'I'll take you home.'

'You needn't——'

'Don't argue, Rochelle,' he snapped. 'I'm not challenging your independence. Apart from believing it a matter of simple courtesy to return a dinner companion to her own front door, my car is still parked outside your house.'

They retraced their steps in silence. Shelley clung to her rage and indignation, seeking more fuel for her anger. She had to go on hating him. She did not dare wonder why.

At her front door she turned to face him. 'Thank you for the meal, Adam,' she said formally. That was all she was thanking him for. The evening as a whole had been a painful disaster. No, it hadn't, part of her argued. The first half had been a delight, until—until she had realised what he was up to. A fox could take lessons in cunning from Adam Trelawney. If only it could have been different. If only they had met—it was too late for that.

'You're welcome.' The open mockery in his reply rekindled her fury. He had never understood. He never would.

'Goodnight,' she said crisply, and turned to unlock the door.

'Just one more thing,' he said.

She withdrew the key and opened the door, glancing round, tone and expression cool. 'What?'

'This,' he muttered and, seizing her shoulders, pulled her roughly against him, his mouth descending on hers in a brutal kiss that stopped her breath and crushed her lips against her teeth. He thrust her away with such suddenness that she staggered and collided with the door-post.

'Goodnight, Rochelle.' His eyes were glittering in the light at the junction of the quay and slip, and his teeth flashed in a brief smile. 'I'll be seeing you.' He climbed into his car and started the engine.

Shelley whirled into the cottage and slammed the door, leaning against it, seething. He was impossible! Arrogant, overbearing, selfish—her hand crept up to touch her swollen mouth. Inexplicably, her eyes filled with tears.

Blinking rapidly, she took off her coat and lay it over the back of the sofa, then dropped her bag on the side-table, her gaze drawn unwillingly to the carnations. Their sweet fragrance filled the room.

Shelley turned her back on them and went to poke some life into the fire, then into the kitchen to make herself a milky drink. She curled up on the sofa, cupping the mug in boths hands as she stared into the dancing flames, her thoughts darting hither and thither like fireflies.

The following day, refreshed by a surprisingly good night's sleep, Shelley arrived at the Gallery to find herself the first one in. Sue arrived a few minutes later and, hanging up her coat, announced that John would not be in, as he had a migraine.

'How rotten for him,' Shelley sympathised. 'He hasn't had one for ages. I suppose it's all the uncertainly that triggered it off.'

'It's one of the difficulties of being an artist,' Sue sighed. 'John is terribly sensitive. He feels things much more keenly than other people.'

How could she know that? Shelley wondered. John certainly aired his feelings more than the rest of them, but were they really so much deeper, or simply more voluble? She merely nodded. What was the point of arguing? It wasn't something anyone could prove. 'I'm sure he'll feel better when we find somewhere else and all this hassle is behind us.'

Sue studied her hands as she twisted her wedding ring round and round. 'Er, well, actually, Shelley, we might not be joining you in a new place. John's been in touch with a friend of his at the Newlyn Art School. Apparently Craig, that's John's friend, is going to America for a year and wants to let his studio and flat.' Excitement crept into Sue's voice. 'Newlyn is famous for its artists, their stuff goes all over the world. If John can just get established down there, who knows what it might lead to?'

Shelley nodded, forcing down her own disappointment. It was all breaking up around her. The hopes and plans they had shared for the Gallery and which she had assumed they would transfer to the new place, when they found it, were dissolving like morning mist. 'That's marvellous, Sue. I'm so glad for you.'

Sue's pale features lit up with a smile of relief. 'Thanks for taking it so well, Sh—Rochelle.'

'Don't you go formal on me,' Shelley said quickly, recalling all too vividly the sound of her name on Adam's lips. 'Let's keep it the way it's always been, please?'

'OK,' Sue agreed, then grimaced. 'I must admit I didn't sleep much last night, worrying about how to tell you.'

Shelley shrugged and pulled her sweater down over her slim hips. 'You have to do whatever's best for you, and it certainly does sound like a marvellous opportunity. Tell John I wish him all the best.'

'Thanks, I will.' Sue was busy stacking boxes of different coloured materials on her table.

'What about your work?' Shelley asked. 'Do you think you'll find an outlet down there?'

Sue nodded. 'Craig says there are several craft shops selling quality goods that will jump at it.' She pulled a face again. 'Good job too, because we'll have to live on whatever I can earn until John starts selling, and the rents aren't cheap. Still,' she brightened, 'it's a challenge.'

'I suppose you'll be going quite soon then,' Shelley said quickly.

'You bet,' Sue grinned. 'We're off to see Craig tomorrow and, all being well, we'll move into the flat next Wednesday.' She looked up, suddenly still, her smile fading. 'I'm sorry, Shelley, I——'

'Forget it,' Shelley interrupted brightly. 'I—I'd better get moving. I've a lot to catch up on.'

Who would be the next to go? she wondered, then ridiculed her own pessimism. In fact, John and Sue's departure might even turn out to be a blessing in disguise. It would surely be easier to find workspace for three, rather than five.

The morning passed in a blur of noise and activity. Customers came and went. A stocky man Shelley knew by sight bought her heron, and as she wrapped it carefully in tissue paper, Shelley felt a pang. Adam had wanted it. Well, so what? What would it have meant to him—another trophy? A reminder of his revenge?

She told Kath and Gary her news at coffee-time during a brief lull in the busy morning, and Shelley read sympathy in Gary's quick glance.

Kath was late back from lunch and seemed to be in a world of her own during the afternoon. But when, at five, they were preparing to close up, she approached Shelley's bench diffidently.

'I—er—won't be in until Wednesday,' she sounded oddly breathless. 'The Woolcraft people are holding an exhibition and sale up at Wadebridge, and I've entered several of my things.'

'Good luck!' Shelley lifted crossed fingers. 'Not that you need it, Kath, your jackets and sweaters are always the first to go.'

'I—I'm staying with my aunt,' Kath blundered on

as though Shelley had not spoken. 'She was widowed last year and she's finding the house a bit much to manage on her own. It's a lovely place, very old, and right in the main street. It's got this super old-fashioned bow window . . . ' She broke off, looking at the floor, then the wall, and finally, her expression a tortured mix of embarrassment and pleading, at Shelley, who was nonplussed, but only for a moment.

Fighting the awful sinking feeling, Shelley managed to school her features into warm interest. She wanted to scream and shout, but what was the point? Kath had already made up her mind. 'I'm sure having you with her for a few days will do your aunt the world of good. Have you thought about the possibility of moving up there permanently? It sounds to me as though she would welcome the company and that window would be perfect for displaying your work.'

Like Sue, Kath visibly sagged with relief. 'Shelley, I'd never have dreamed of leaving here, and all of you, if everything had been all right. But now the Gallery's been sold . . . ' She shrugged awkwardly.

'I understand.' Shelley forced a smile, though her jaws ached and her throat was stiff with misery. 'You couldn't be in a better spot. With the Royal Cornwall Show there in June, I expect you'll get enough orders to keep you busy for the next five years.'

Gary caught up with her as she was hurrying down the street. 'Hey, what's the rush? Got a date or something?'

'No!' Shelley's tone was so sharp, Gary blinked, clearly startled. 'I'm sorry.' She shook her head and tried to grin. 'God, what a day!'

'You know the old saying about rats and a sinking ship,' Gary snorted with rare venom.

Shelley touched his hand. 'We can't blame them, Gary.' She tilted her head to one side. 'Give it to me straight. I may as well know the worst. Have you got something else lined up?'

Gary turned his hand over and snatched her fingers, squeezing them so tightly, Shelley almost winced. 'I'm with you, Shell, all the way. We'll find somewhere soon, I know we will. Look, let's go to the King's for a drink. I picked up some more stuff from the estate agent's at lunchtime. There might be something just right for us.'

'You're on.' Shelley smiled. 'But first could I have my fingers back? It will take a week to straighten them out again.'

Gary went pink and apologised, stuffing his hands in the pockets of his donkey-jacket.

In the dimly lit lounge bar, sitting side by side on a bench shaped like a church pew with a red leatherette seat, they pored over the details of shops for sale or rent.

'It's no good,' Shelley said at last, heaving a deep sigh as she picked up her tomato juice from the half-barrel that served as a table, 'I don't see how we can afford any of them.'

'Shell,' Gary half turned towards her, 'look, don't get mad, but isn't there any chance at all of your family helping out? Just a loan,' he added hurriedly, seeing her expression tighten. 'I do mean a loan, Shell, all legal, but at a lower interest rate maybe——'

'No,' she said with quiet finality. 'They wouldn't do it, and in any case, I couldn't ask. You'll just have to accept it, Gary.'

He shrugged and picked up his beer. 'Oh, well,' he grinned crookedly, 'it was just a thought.'

She nodded and stood up, aware of his curiosity. 'I'd better get on home now. Thanks for the drink.'

His face fell. 'Must you? I thought maybe we could get a take-away. My treat,' he added hastily and grinned. 'I sold a briefcase today.' His grin faded, 'I mean, there's still a lot to discuss.'

Shelley shook her head. 'I don't think I can face any more today.'

Gary stood up. 'Is he waiting for you?' He spoke so softly, Shelley wasn't sure she had heard correctly. But his quick, half ashamed glanced proved that she had.

Fighting a sudden spurt of anger and impatience, she answered gently, 'No. I'm going home alone, to an empty house. I'm tired and I don't want to talk any more, to anyone.'

Gary fumbled for her hand. 'Don't be cross, Shell,' he begged. 'I can't help it. I think the world of you, how can I compete——?'

'Who asked you to?' she cut in, her voice low and barely controlled. 'Adam Trelawney is very much in the past.' A vivid recollected of his brutal kiss and parting words, *'I'll be seeing you,'* sent an icy shiver down her spine. No, she vowed, never again.

'You call last night the past?' Gary muttered. 'I saw you both, going into the Waterfront. It didn't look like you were mad with him. Smiling, you were.'

'Then you should have hung around,' she retorted. 'Things were certainly different when we came out.' Shelley wrapped both arms around his. 'Gary, don't go jealous on me. There's no need. You're my closest friend, believe me. I need you right now.'

He opened his mouth to say something, but changed his mind and patted her hand where she clung to him. 'Come on, I'll walk you home. When am I going to see your holiday snaps?'

Grateful for his good nature, and relieved to get off the subject of Adam, Shelley's smile held more warmth and promise than she realised 'I should have them back by Tuesday. Tell you what, I'll bring them with me when I come for that meal. Lord knows how they'll turn out! Still they should be good for a laugh. I had to ask all sorts of strangers to help when I wanted one of me. The camel driver took two then charged me for his assistance!'

Gary grinned. 'Mum'll go spare. She couldn't believe

it when I told her you'd gone abroad on your own.'

Shelley glanced at him, smiling. 'Lots of girls do, Gary.'

'Yes, but they're usually—well, you know.'

Shelley was puzzled. 'No, I don't know. They're usually what?'

He looked slightly uncomfortable. 'What Mum would call no better than they should be. You know, on the hunt.'

Shelley's chin came up, all trace of amusement wiped from her face. 'Really? And is that what she thinks I was doing? Hunting?

'No, Shell,' Gary sounded shocked. 'of course not. Mum knows you're not like that. I told her you just needed a complete rest and some sunshine. She thought you were taking an awful risk, that's all. She was worried about you?'

Shelley's shoulders slumped. She was far too wound up. If she wasn't careful she'd end up saying something she'd regret. 'That was kind of her, but quite unnecessary. I can take care of myself.'

'You don't have to, Shell,' Gary blurted, colouring. 'I mean, I'm here.'

She squeezed his arm. 'I don't know what I'd do without you, Gary.' She kissed him lightly on the cheek. 'I'll see you on Monday.' Slipping her arm from his, she gave him a brief wave and, leaving him standing, a hunched, hopeful figure with both hands thrust deep in his pockets, she ran down the slip and on to the quay.

As she moved about the cottage, catching up on chores, the scent of Adam's carnations followed her. She didn't want to think about him. The scars were not as healed as she had thought. But it was hard to force the sound of his voice and the memory of his harsh features from her mind with the flowers as a constant reminder.

She couldn't simply throw them away. Wilful

destruction of beauty was beyond her. Impulsively, she snatched them out of their vase and, carrying them, dripping, into the kitchen, wrapped the long stems in two paper towels.

'They're making me sneeze,' she said to a surprised Elsie as she thrust the blooms at her. Without waiting for a reply, she hurried back into her cottage and firmly closed the door.

Emptying the vase, she put it away, then took her washing out of the tumble drier and set up the ironing board where she could watch a nature programme on TV.

Half-way through, she heard the throaty purr of Adam's car. She froze, her heart hammering against her ribs. The smell of scorching made her snatch the iron off a cotton skirt. With a muffled gasp she clattered the iron down on to its metal stand and seizing the skirt, examined it, straining to hear what was happening outside.

The car door clunked shut. Shelley held her breath, waiting for his knock. Why had he come back? What could he possibly want with her? Surely they had said everything there was to say last night?

Though she expected it, the sound of his knuckles on her door made her jump, but she remained rooted to the spot. She wouldn't answer. She wouldn't open it. He had no right to come barging back into her life, demanding entry to her home, taking up her time.

He knocked again, louder. She swallowed, clutching the crumpled skirt. He had wanted an explanation and he had got it. Why had he come back? Why didn't he just leave her alone?'

'Oh, 'tis you, Mr Trelawney.' She heard Elsie's voice. 'I know she's in fer she were round 'ere jest a few minutes since. Try the door, why don't 'ee,' Elsie suggested. 'Tell 'ee what, I'll do it for 'ee.'

Realising what a fool she would look if Adam took Elsie at her word, Shelley let out the breath she had been holding in a shaky rush and started towards the door just as it opened.

As soon as he caught sight of her, Adam withdrew his head, while keeping his hand firmly on the handle, and the door ajar. Shelley heard him call to Elsie, 'It's all right, Mrs Penfold, you go along in out of the cold. I'll see you tomorrow morning.' His tone brooked no argument and as he waited for Elsie to close her door, Shelley could not help a momentary smile. She would lay odds that Elsie's curiosity had never been aroused or cut off quite so effectively before.

Adam stepped inside the cottage, remembering to duck his head beneath the low lintel. Suddenly the room seemed smaller.

They stared at one another. Adam's glance flicked briefly to the side-table, now bare, and one dark brow lifted fractionally, but he did not ask about the flowers.

Shelley felt warm colour climb her throat like a tide but kept her chin high. 'Did you want something?'

'Yes,' he drawled. 'You.'

The words hit her like a clenched fist in the stomach. She felt literally winded.

'To come with me to see some restoration work I'm doing,' he added, and she knew his phrasing had been deliberate and that he had not missed her instantly controlled reaction.

'Th-this is hardly the time——' she began sharply, her anger directed at much as herself as at him. He was toying with her like a cat with a mouse, and she was so strung up she was playing right into his hands.

'Not right now,' His mild exasperation was a further blow to her self-esteem. 'Tomorrow.'

'No, thank you,' she rejected flatly.

'I must insist. ' He smiled and it had the deadly quality of a barracuda. 'You have branded me a destroyer, a vandal who made his fortune out of tearing and despoiling beautiful buildings. Surely I have the right of reply?' A steely quality crept into his tone. 'Or are you so full of self-pity that justice and a fair hearing for others don't count any more?'

Shelley gasped. 'How dare you? After what you've done in the past two weeks——'

'I'll pick you up at ten.'

'I haven't said——'

'As soon as I've had a look at Mrs Penfold's damp wall,' he went on calmly.

Shelley was still desperately fighting a rearguard action. 'If it's a long way——'

'It isn't,' he cut her short. 'But lunch might be a good idea. I'll bring it.' Without another word he walked out, leaving Shelley staring at the closed door.

CHAPTER FIVE

AT NINE-THIRTY the following morning Shelley was still telling herself she would not go. She would apologise for any misjudgements she had been guilty of, but as for spending the day with him—masochism wasn't her scene.

Adam Trelawney meant nothing but trouble. Her carefully rebuilt life was crumbling around her, her friends were leaving, and her work was in jeopardy, all because of him. And worse, much worse, he still had the power to attract her.

She shook out her duvet with unaccustomed violence, then finished tidying her bedroom. Outside, gulls shrieked and swooped as the sun streamed in through curtains of cream, flower-sprigged cotton and filled the room with golden light.

Just as she closed the window Adam's car drew up outside. Her heart tripped on a double-beat and she caught her lower lip between her teeth as he got out. The fresh, gusty breeze tumbled his thick hair, tossing the black curls across his forehead. Wearing an Icelandic sweater over a navy sports shirt, dark blue trainers, and faded jeans that clung to his long legs, outlining the muscular contours of his thighs, he looked more relaxed than Shelley had ever seen him.

As if aware of her scrutiny he glanced up. It was too late for her to duck back out of sight. She waited for his sardonic, knowing smile that was almost a sneer. But it didn't come. His teeth flashed in a cheerful grin and he raised one hand, the fingers spread, and mouthed the words 'five minutes', then

moved round the car to Elsie's door, which opened
before his knuckles made contact.

Shelley stared at her reflection in the dressing-table
mirror and pressed her palms to her flushed cheeks.
What was she to do? Last night he had accused her
of not caring about justice or fair play. That was rich,
coming from him! And if she went with him it would
be the third time in as many days he had demanded
—and got—his own way.

On the other hand, if she *did* accompany him this
one last time, and let him show her the work he was
doing, it would prove his charges were unfounded and
that she did indeed possess the very qualities he
accused her of lacking. Then he would have no further
excuse to bother her. She would be free to start
rebuilding a life shattered *for the second time* by Adam
Trelawney. Free? her inner voice mocked. But she
shut it out, refusing to listen. There was nothing else
for it. She would *have* to go.

Shelley ignored the tiny frisson of pleasure that
shivered through her as Adam opened the passenger
door of the Daimler for her to get in. She wasn't there
to enjoy herself, merely to prove a point and then get
him out of her life once and for all.

As he switched on the ignition and the engine
purred into life, he glanced at her. It was brief, but
all-encompassing, and Shelley knew that nothing about
her appearance had escaped him, from her hair, falling
loose about the shawl collar of the Arran jacket she
had put on for warmth over her beige and brown
checked shirt, to her dark brown cords tucked into
ankle boots.

'Did you knit that?'

'Yes.' Again she waited, but he said nothing more.
In fact, he made no effort to talk during the entire
journey which both surprised and irritated her, to
begin with. She had expected him at least to say where
they were going. But she had more sense than to ask,

realising that had he wanted her to know he'd have told her. So, it was to be a mystery trip.

He slotted in a tape, adjusted the volume so that the strains of Vivaldi's *The Four Seasons* issued soft yet clear from the car's stereo system, and set the Daimler on to the road out of town.

Shelley shot him a swift glance but his attention was on the road, and though his fingers beat lightly on the steering wheel, she could read nothing in his expression.

Was it simply coincidence or had he chosen the music deliberately? More memories crowded her mind. The Royal Festival Hall on the bank of the Thames, she and Adam listening to this same piece played by the London Symphony Orchestra. Afterwards they had walked through quiet, rain-washed streets to a little bistro for supper. That had been in the early days, when they were just beginning to get to know one another. It seemed so long ago, almost another lifetime. She still had the record at home, though she hadn't played it for a very long time.

The anxiety that had strained her nerves and held her muscles tense began to drain away. Whether it was due to the music, or to the early spring sunshine illuminating snowdrops and primroses in the hedgerow and dancing on the blue waters of the estuary, or even Adam's silence, Shelley neither knew nor cared. She settled more comfortably into the deep leather seat. If she had to go through with this, it seemed only sensible to try and enjoy it.

It wasn't until they actually turned into the drive that Shelley realised their destination. She sat forward as he slowed the car to halt at the side of the Georgian house.

'*This* is it? You're working *here*?'

He nodded. 'It's a beautiful property, but has been badly neglected.'

'It's not surprising really.' Shelley eyed the flaking

walls behind the network of scaffolding. 'The cost of maintaining a place like this must be frightening. Still, the new owner can obviously afford it. Whoever it is must be an outsider. I can't imagine anyone local being able . . . '

To her surprise, Adam didn't wait for her to finish before opening his door and getting out. 'I'll show you around outside first,' he said over his shoulder then squinted up at the sky. 'It looks as if there's rain on the way.'

Shelley peered through the windscreen. A thin, translucent veil now covered the sun, and grey clouds with rough-torn edges were piling in from the south-west. She raised her eyebrows, and her mouth curved in a sceptical smile. 'Since when have you been able to read weather signs?'

He leaned in to answer her. 'Since Matt and Terry Treloar took me oyster fishing,' he retorted airily and, straightening up, shut the door.

Shelley jumped out quickly. Staring at him across the highly polished roof, she declared, 'Come on, Adam, everyone round here knows the Treloar brothers never take *anyone* else on the *Lily*. I can't see them breaking a twenty-year habit for a landlubber from London who wouldn't know a mainsail from a mizzen.'

Adam's slow smile and hooded glance had a peculiar effect on Shelley's breathing. 'I can be very persuasive,' he said softly, then set off towards the lower garden, leaving Shelley with no choice but to follow. 'They took me round Black Rock and across to St Just, then up the estuary to test my ability to stand up to race conditions, though for half the time I was shifting ballast and didn't even get a look over the gunwhale.'

Shelley compressed her lips on a grin.

'I repaid them by helping Matt with a few days' dredging while Terry was laid up with a sprained ankle.'

Before she could say anything else, he held his hand out and Shelley saw callouses and newly healed blisters across his palm. She shook her head, utterly bewildered. 'But . . . why?'

He gazed out across the harbour. 'I'm thinking of buying a workboat.'

'You're *what*?' Shelley was stunned. 'What on earth for?'

Adam shrugged and pushed his hands into his jeans pockets. 'Tradition, I suppose. Workboats have dredged oysters in this estuary for almost two centuries. The continuity and sense of history in that appeals to me. It's one of the reasons I really enjoy the restoration and preservation aspect of my work.' He moved on down the overgrown path, stepping over the puddles left by overnight rain.

Shelley stared after him, recalling his surprise at her ability to make chutney, and her own reply. 'There's a lot about me you don't know,' she had said, mentally accusing him of not caring enough to find out. Now it was she who was learning, and suddenly he was even more of a stranger.

'But—but how on earth are you going to find time to do both?' she queried.

'I don't intend to *work* the boat,' he replied patiently. 'The dredging season finishes in a week or so at the end of March. In any case, even though I wouldn't pose much of a threat, not knowing where the oyster beds are, trying to muscle in on their livelihood wouldn't exactly endear me to the locals.'

'Why should you care?' Shelley retorted tightly, thinking of the Gallery and of her own ruined plans and hopes. 'You won't be around long enough for it to matter what they think. Once you've built your block of flats you'll be off back to the bright lights of London.'

He glanced over his shoulder at her. 'Do you know,' he mused, 'that sounds as though you might miss me.'

'Miss you?' Shelley spluttered, flushing hotly. 'A lifetime apart wouldn't be long enough! Anyway,' she rushed on anxious to steer the conversation on to a far less personal track, 'what *do* you want the boat for?' His behaviour, in fact his whole attitude, was quite different to that of the past three days and, while admittedly more pleasant, it was also unsettling. For she was finding it ever more difficult to remember all the reasons she had for hating him.

'I'm going to race her.'

This time Shelley did laugh. She simply couldn't help it. Adam's swift frown sobered her, then he too grinned, flexing his broad shoulders.

'I'll win before the summer's over,' he promised.

'Oh, of course,' Shelley agreed ironically, even as it dawned on her that Adam clearly intended to remain here for six months at least.

'Do you want to bet on it?' he challenged.

Shelley shook her head. 'It would be like taking sweets from a child.'

'Scared you might lose?' he taunted.

'You have to be joking. *You* beat men with the sea in their blood? Men who have worked and raced their boats in these waters since they were children?'

'Well then?'

Stung by his arrogance, by the sheer audacity of his claim, she hesitated only an instant. 'You're on. Name the stakes.' And regretted the rashly impulsive words the instant she had spoken.

His eyes gleamed beneath heavy lids. 'I'll give it some thought,' he said softly, and before Shelley could back out or protest, he changed the subject completely, making a sweeping movement with one arm. 'This garden was once famous for its camellias and rhododendrons.' He indicated the overgrown shrubbery. 'I have two men starting work tomorrow on clearing the brambles and bracken. The drive will have to be weeded and sprayed before the new chippings go down and we'll need a Gravely to tackle that grass. But it shouldn't take too long to restore the lawns.'

Shelley grimaced as she surveyed the tangled undergrowth and the bright orange and yellow trumpets of daffodils standing in proud clusters within a cage of bramble and creeper. 'I wouldn't have thought that was your responsibility. Surely the owner——'

'House and garden are an entity,' he replied. 'It would be pointless doing one without the other.'

'Yes, but why——?'

He didn't wait to hear her question. 'Come and look at this. There's even a slipway down to the water. I'm told there was a boat-house once, but there's nothing left of it now. Careful!' He caught her round the waist as her smooth-soled boot skidded on the sloping muddy path.

Instinctively, Shelley clutched at him. A quick glance over the edge revealed a ten foot drop on to jagged rocks below. Quite far enough for her to have broken an ankle or sustained deep cuts from the uptilted layers of razor-sharp stone.

Adam drew her forward on to a drier part of the path. 'OK?' The question was casual, laconic.

Shelley nodded, 'Fine,' but her heart thudded sickeningly. Was it reaction to the near-accident, or to his arm around her? That strong, familiar arm that had promised closeness and security, until she awoke to the fact that it was also a shackle, holding her back from fulfilment in her own career.

'Can you see where the continuous force of the waves has undermined the foundations and broken away chunks from the slip?'

She nodded again. She had let go of his shoulder and was standing beside and a little in front of him. He seemed to have forgotten that his arm still rested lightly around her waist as he pointed with his free hand to twisted, rusty iron bars protruding from the sand-coloured concrete. But she was acutely conscious of it as she tried to concentrate on what he was saying.

'I'm tempted to restore the slip with local stone rather than new concrete,' he mused. 'It would be more in keeping with the property. What do you think?'

She glanced up and saw that his eyes held a strange light and the last traces of humour had vanished from his sensual mouth. His hand was warm on the curve of her hip and her shoulder rested lightly against his chest.

She was vividly aware of him as a man, a tall, dark, potently attractive man. He had never worn his masculinity like a badge. It was not, as with so many, a deliberately cultivated image, but an integral part of him. Men seemed automatically to defer to him, while women fluttered and preened beneath his amused gaze. But there was no vanity in his make-up, simply an acceptance of his own power. And its effect on her had been devastating.

When her father had brought Adam home and she met him again for the first time since childhood, she had been all the things of which her mother despaired —serious, determined and naïve. With gentleness and humour Adam had awakened in her girlish body a woman's sensuality, and in her heart a love that had turned to bitterness and hatred.

Hot colour flooded her face like a tide and, aware of his eyes on the pulse beating rapidly at the base of her throat, Shelley broke free and walked forward a few paces, pretending to take a closer look at the slipway.

Was she out of her mind? That was long past, over and done with. But his touch stirred so many memories, and though her head told her nothing had changed, that he had brought her here simply to prove a point, and that *her* work meant as little to him now as it had then, her body yearned for him.

'Yes, that's a good idea,' she agreed hastily, and

turned towards the house, oddly breathless. 'What are you going to do about the jackdaws?' She pointed to the chattering birds bobbing and bowing on the chimney-pots. 'They'll start nesting soon.'

It was the first genuine laugh she had heard from him since he had confirmed her deepest fears by appearing in the Gallery. She spun round, her eyes wide with uncertainty.

'Agreeing with me, Rochelle? Whatever next?'

There was a weakness in the pit of her stomach as she faced his mocking smile. It was on the tip of her tongue to retort that her thoughts had been elsewhere, but she bit the words back just in time. With his uncanny perception he would realise almost at once that she had been distracted by their physical contact, and that would be tantamount to giving him the bullets with which to shoot her.

She shrugged, extravagantly casual, her palms damp. 'On this occasion you happen to be right.'

Though he still smiled, his expression was sceptical and his grey eyes shrewd. She shivered. 'Fantastic view, isn't it?' He gestured widely, indicating the whole of the town on the far side of the river, from the headland, along the waterfront and hill behind, up to the bridge.

Shelley nodded, raising both hands to shield her eyes from the glare of the veiled sun. 'I've never seen my—the cottages from this angle before,' she said, letting him know she hadn't forgotten the property was his. But speaking of her home prompted a question that had been hovering on the edge of her mind for a couple of days. 'Where are you staying, Adam?'

'Why do you ask?' His tone was light, but the question had clearly taken him by surprise.

She lowered her hands and eyed him briefly. 'Just curious. But it's none of my business, is it?' She looked away, frustration rising like bile in her throat. He had managed, one way or another, to find out almost

everything about her present life. He had even had a
good look around her home. But she knew less about
him now than three years ago. A drop of rain splashed
on to her cheek.

'Time to go inside,' he announced. 'As for the rest,
you're not missing much. The kitchen garden, behind
that wall, is a wilderness, and over there,' he pointed
to a tangle of wisteria and honeysuckle vines which
almost obscured a small wooden shack, half-open at
the front, 'the floor of the summer-house has rotted
out, so it's not safe to visit. Not this time, anyway.'

Shelley kept her head down, concentrating on where
she was putting her feet amid the undergrowth. Surely
he wasn't implying there would be a 'next time'?

Adam stepped up on to an ornamental wall
supporting a terrace which brought them back to the
level of the house. 'About the jackdaws—the chimneys
will be capped with wire mesh this week.'

The top of the wall was slippery with moss and
lichen, and as she stepped up he grasped her upper
arm to steady her. 'I don't want roasted nestlings any
more than I want newly painted rooms full of smoke.'

Shelley gritted her teeth at the implied rebuke and,
just before she could pull free, Adam let go of her
arm and they crossed the drive to the front door.

A flat-topped porch supported by four once-white
columns on granite plinths shielded it from the weather.
Shelley glanced back, seeing the clouds coming in
lower and fat drops of rain beginning to fall with
increasing speed.

Reluctantly, Shelley had to admit she was impressed.
Not just by the house which, despite its bare, neglected
state, was even more beautiful than she imagined, but
also by Adam's enthusiasm for the restoration project.

The re-wiring had been completed and new plumbing
installed. In the kitchen a new Aga with a copper
hood and extractor was in place, and on either side
hand-made oak units were in the process of being

installed. Terracotta quarry-tiles covered the floor and Shelley knew that the large, airy room would be a joy to work in, cool in summer, warm and cosy in winter.

She had been unable to suppress a gasp when Adam showed her the champagne-coloured circular bath sunk into a raised surround formed by wide shallow steps ready for carpeting.

'Why don't you try it for size?' Adam suggested as she stared at it.

'I can't swim,' she said drily. 'It looks big enough for a whole family.'

'Hardly,' he demurred. 'But two people could be very comfortable. It can be used as an ordinary tub, or as a jacuzzi. Very sociable, double bathing.'

'I wouldn't know,' Shelley retorted and, feeling her cheeks burn at his open mockery, she marched back through the bedroom with its separate dressing area and magnificent views of the harbour and estuary.

'Of course, central heating is a necessity,' he explained as they descended the curving staircase and he led the way through the double doors into the drawing-room. 'I thought about using solar energy and hiding the panels on the inner pitch of the roof, but it isn't feasible for a house this size.'

Shelley stared at him. This man talking about conservation and non-pollutant energy was the same man who intended tearing down her beloved Gallery to build a block of holiday flats. Would she ever understand him?'

He crossed to one of the two long windows that reached almost to floor level and, pushing his hands into his pockets, stared out at the rain. 'Mind you,' he went on, 'if I ever decide to build a swimming pool in the kitchen garden, I shall use solar energy to heat the water.'

As his words sank into her consciousness like pebbles in a pool, their ripples spreading wider and wider, Shelley stopped breathing. He couldn't mean—he *couldn't!* And yet it would explain his evasiveness, his reluctance to let her ask questions.

'Adam,' her throat was so dry her voice emerged as a husky whisper. She swallowed and tried again. 'Adam, who owns this house?'

He turned slowly from the window, perfectly at ease. 'I do.'

'Why didn't you tell me?' Shelley demanded furiously.

He shrugged. 'You never asked. Anyway, what difference does it make? You agreed to come and see a house I'm restoring. All right, I happen to own it. So what? I assure you the standard of workmanship will be exactly the same as in any of the other properties I've restored.'

'I bet it will,' Shelley almost spat.

Adam glanced at his watch. 'Time for lunch, I think.'

'No, thank you,' Shelley replied at once.

'Well, I'm hungry,' Adam made for the door, 'and you'll change your mind when you see what I've brought.'

'I don't want your food. I want to go home.'

'I'll just fetch the hamper,' Adam said evenly. 'I won't be a moment.'

'Didn't you hear me?' Shelley shouted. 'I want to go home!' She flinched as Adam suddenly swung round, his face set like stone.

'Rochelle, the front door is open. You can leave any time you like. Just remember it's Sunday, there are no buses, it's pouring with rain, and you face a four-mile walk back to town. But if that's what you really want, then you go right ahead.'

Shelley stared at him, taken aback. 'You mean you'd make me *walk* home?'

He stood squarely in front of the doorway, his feet apart, arms folded. 'I'm not *making* you do anything,' he said flatly. 'I invited you here, you came. You're free to leave any time you like, but *I'm* not ready to go yet. You please yourself.' His voice roughened in disgust. 'It's about par for the course.' He turned and wrenched open the double doors.

Shelley's chin came up. 'What is that supposed to mean?' she snapped.

He looked over his shoulder. 'You have this unfortunate habit of running away from anything that upsets you. You'll live to regret it, Rochelle, for life has a way of catching up and getting even.' He strode out, leaving her staring after him.

She was still there, trapped in a mire of doubt and uncertainty when he returned a few moments later carrying a wicker picnic hamper and the thick, tartan car-rug from the back seat of the Daimler. Raindrops glistened on his sweater and in his black hair.

Shelley clasped her upper arms as if holding herself together. 'Are you threatening me?' She fought to keep her voice steady.

'Oh, are you still here?' His tone was cool and distant. The truce, the easy atmosphere, had vanished like water in a desert, and though it was all Adam's fault for not telling her the truth straight away, Shelley mourned its loss.

'Well? Are you?' she demanded.

He had spread the rug on the floor, opened the hamper, and was setting out fine china plates, silver cutlery and two crystal wine goblets. 'What possible motive could I have for threatening you?'

He shot her an impatient glance.

Shelley shrugged helplessly. 'I don't know. Why have you come down here? Why have you bought this house?'

He opened various containers to reveal thick slices of cold roast chicken, tubs of mixed salad, crusty granary rolls and butter, a jar of mayonnaise and a bottle of white wine wrapped in a spotless napkin.

In spite of her emotional turmoil, Shelley found her

mouth watering at the spread. She hadn't been able
to face much breakfast, and the stress of spending the
morning with Adam, pleasant though much of it had
been, had burned up her store of nervous energy. She
was cold and ravenously hungry.

'If you've decided to stay, then for goodness' sake
sit down,' Adam commanded. 'You look like the
spectre at the feast.'

'Thanks,' she snapped, but did as he said, pointedly
settling on the edge of the rug farthest from him.

There was a loud pop then a gentle gurgle as he
uncorked and poured the wine. He handed her a
goblet and, as she took it, Shelley was careful to avoid
any contact between their hands. He lifted his own.
'To changes,' he announced cryptically and, holding
her gaze, drank without waiting for her reply. 'Help
yourself,' he offered, indicating the food and beginning
to fork chicken on to his own plate.

Shelley set down her glass and buttered a roll. 'How
did you manage all this?'

'The hamper is mine,' Adam answered, spooning
apple, walnut and celery salad on to his plate. 'It's
vital for the amount of travelling I do. I can stop
when and where I like, and avoid motorway service
stations. The hotel I'm staying at supplied the food
and wine.'

Shelley swallowed a mouthful, and immediately felt
stronger. 'You're not living here yet, then?' She
couldn't have said why, but that made her feel
somehow less threatened. She thought of spiders and
flies and had to suppress a totally unexpected grin.
Her nerves really were in a bit of a state.

He shook his head. 'I was tempted, that view . . . '
He lifted his head and gazed towards the window,
then shrugged. 'But without water, electricity or even
the chance to light a fire until the chimneys had been
swept, I decided against it. I'm staying at the King's
Arms.'

Shelley knew the place. Situated just off the main road half-way between the mansion and the town, it was an old coaching inn. While retaining all the genuine charm of its origins, the interior was quietly luxurious and its food was famous far beyond Cornwall.

'I'm rather surprised at your small-mindedness,' Adam said conversationally.

Shelley bristled at his arrogance, but managed to assume an expression of polite interest, recognising his remark as deliberately provocative. 'Is that a general criticism,' she asked sweetly, 'or are you referring to something in particular?'

'What difference can it possibly make to you that I have decided to buy a house down here?' Adam demanded, watching her closely.

'Before I answer that, tell me why you did,' Shelley shot back.

Adam lifted one shoulder. 'It's a beautiful area, I like the locals, the pace of life is slower, just the antidote I need to the pressures of London.'

'There are other places with all those attributes,' Shelley countered.

'Not with a harbour like this for sailing, nor with the workboat tradition,' he replied at once. 'Besides, since Nicholas's death I have a vested interest in this town and, as landlord to several sitting tenants, it's my duty to ensure the properties are maintained.'

'By them or by you?' Shelley was openly sceptical, but the withering effect was somewhat spoiled by her mouthful of chicken.

'By me,' he answered soberly. 'But that's beside the point. You are apparently doing what you want to do. You have made a comfortable home for yourself and established a new life. Why shouldn't I do the same? Of course, you are hiding behind another name, but I suppose you can't help your lack of courage.'

'If I'd been as much of a coward as you seem to

think,' Shelley hit back fiercely, 'I'd never have had
the guts to leave. I would have stayed and gone
through with the charade. It wasn't easy, Adam, and
it wasn't done on impulse. I altered my name because
I had to prove to myself I could make it on my own.
I needed to cut all links with the past, to be accepted
for myself, not for my family's wealth and social
position, and certainly not because I happened to be
the daughter of one famous man, and the ex-fiancée
of another.' She took a long gulp of wine, clutching
the glass with white-knuckled fingers, and feeling the
sparkling liquid warm her stomach and rock the room
slightly.

'Were you afraid I'd follow you?' Adam asked.

Misled by his mild, almost off-hand tone, Shelley
hesitated, then nodded.

Adam's expression hardened. 'Then you went to a
lot of trouble for nothing,' his voice was steel-edged.
'After all, by running away as you did, you made it
perfectly clear that I meant nothing to you, but you
just didn't have the guts to tell me so.'

'That's not true!' Shelley flared, all caution tossed
aside, caring only that he saw the truth as *she* had
seen it. 'I *loved* you, Adam.' A flash of triumph crossed
his face, so swift, so fleeting, Shelley did not recognise
it for what it was until much, much later. Wounded
by his bitter accusation, determined to refute it, she
gave no thought to the consequences of her confession.
'You were the first . . . the only man I . . . had
ever loved. But you—you were taking over my life. I
felt suffocated, Adam!'

His face was bleak and his eyes glittered. 'So instead
of discussing how you felt with me, you simply packed
up and left.'

'You were never *there* to talk to,' Shelley hurled the
words at him, all the loneliness and despair she had
suffered then spilling out. 'You spent more time with
my parents than you did with me. There were business

meetings and conferences, discussions with lawyers, and bankers, just you and my father. Then you'd be away for a week at a time inspecting properties. My mother was planning the wedding and my father annexed you the instant you came into the house. It was *my* life you were all busily organising, yet no one would listen to me. You were all too busy. The only time we saw each other in those last few months was at dinner parties. Hardly the place for a serious conversation. And when you *did* talk to me, it was mostly to remind me of my future career as housewife, hostess and mother of your children.' She broke off, her chest heaving as though she had just completed a long and difficult ordeal.

Their meal forgotten, the debris pushed aside, they faced each other, oblivious to the rain hammering on the windows and the rising wind whipping up waves in the harbour and keening through the bare branches of the oaks behind the summer-house.

'Was the thought of being my wife and bearing my children so abhorrent then?' he grated.

'*No!*' she cried, 'but it wasn't the whole of my ambition either. I had a career too, but that was just ignored. All of you were so used to organising, to making decisions, you seemed to forget there was someone else involved—me. I was being crushed by the three of you, and I knew that if I gave in and let it happen, I would cease to exist as an individual. For the rest of my life I would be somebody's daughter, somebody's wife, and somebody's mother.'

Shelley glanced down at her clasped hands, then back at the man whose dark, intent gaze had never left her face. 'You didn't need me, Adam. You had no time for the things that really mattered in my life. Any woman with the right background would have suited you.'

She gasped as he lunged forward and seized her wrist, jerking her off-balance so that she sprawled full-length on the rug. Swift as a striking cobra he twisted round, leaning over her, supporting his weight on his hands planted either side of her head.

'You don't believe that,' he hissed, 'you can't!' Shelley had never seen him so angry. He was literally trembling with rage and there was a whiteness round his nostrils and mouth that frightened her. 'There were other women before you, of course there were, but I never wanted to *marry* any of them.'

'But—my father——' she began.

'Your father had nothing to do with it,' he cut in, his voice a whipcrack. 'His schemes and the family fortunes didn't matter a damn to me, except as security for you. Once I'd seen what the skinny little ten-year-old I remembered had grown into, what happened next was *my* decision, no one else's.'

'Why should I believe you?' she croaked. 'How can you expect me to? I didn't know how you felt, you never told me. You never even——' She flushed scarlet and turned her head, not bold enough to say the words that would lay bare the aching need she had felt for him, the longing for reassurance that only his kisses and the touch of his hands on her body could give. But she was not quick enough to avoid the swift perception in his smoky eyes, and her skin burned.

'Made love to you?' he rasped. 'In God's name, Rochelle, what did you take me for? I knew you were a virgin.'

'Was it so obvious?' she asked bitterly.

'Yes,' he replied, his tone suddenly gentle, 'and that is no criticism. I also knew that, once awakened, you would be a sensual, passionate woman. And because I wanted everything to be right for you, no secrecy, no feelings of guilt or shame, I was prepared to wait until *after* the wedding. Why do you think I kept myself so busy. It wasn't *lack* of interest in that slender body of yours.' Hot colour flooded Shelley's face once more. 'Just the opposite. I wanted you so badly I was finding it almost impossible to keep my hands off you.'

'But *I* didn't know. You never told me,' Shelley whispered hoarsely, trying but failing to tear her gaze from the changing shadows in his heavy-lidded eyes.

'What the hell was I supposed to say?' he growled.

'So it's different for you, is it?' Shelley challenged, attempting to ignore the dangerous excitement sliding through her veins like a drug.

His dark brows drew together. 'What do you mean?'

'Didn't it ever occur to you that I would worry? That I would think there was something wrong? That I would jump to precisely the conclusion I did—that you didn't really love me, after all, you had never said you did, and your proposal was nothing more than a business arrangement between you and my father?'

Hostility welled up in Shelley. She had suffered deeply since her flight three years ago, going over it all in her mind a million times, racked with guilt, even though in the circumstances she had had no choice. 'How *dare* you cloak yourself in righteous indignation and accuse me of running away from my problems! What were *you* doing?'

Seething with fury and resentment, she started to scramble up, wanting only to get away from him, desperate to break the insidious spell their physical closeness was weaving despite the antipathy that crackled like electricity between them.

He grabbed her shoulder and forced her back again, his body half-covering hers as he used his weight to hold her down.

Shelley could neither move nor breathe. Pinned to the floor, her bones melted as the ripple of desire that hardened his body echoed within her. Their eyes locked, their faces scarcely inches apart. A spasm crossed Adam's face. His lips drew back, baring his teeth, and his sharp intake of breath was a soft hiss. His head came down, blotting out the light and in

that final second, with a wordless moan, Shelley tried
to turn her head aside.

Adam growled deep in his throat and pressed his
lips to the soft skin below her ear, a scalding touch
that sent an exquisite tremor through her. She gasped,
her heart pounding violently, and jerked away, but
this time he was ready. His mouth covered hers and
she was swept away on a dark, swelling tide.

CHAPTER SIX

SHELLEY hugged the soft folds of her dressing-gown around her. Hunched in the cushioned window-seat in her bedroom, the curtains pulled back, she drew her knees up, resting her elbows on them as she stared across the river.

She had deliberately stayed up late, finding jobs to keep her busy, until she ached with tiredness. Even then her sleep had been fitful, her dreams vivid and disturbing.

Glancing at her watch, Shelley realised she had been sitting there for almost an hour. Dawn had broken, its pearly light heralding the birth of a new day. But she could only look back, still haunted by what had happened seventeen hours ago.

Why had she stayed, instead of leaving before lunch as instinct warned her? The discomfort of a long walk in the pouring rain would have been a small price to pay compared with the confusion and bitter shame that filled her now.

How could she have allowed—no, not allowed —*welcomed* his hungry embrace? Her skin tingled and a delicious weakness infused every nerve as she relived his burning kisses. His lips had explored every contour of her face and throat. His mouth had savoured hers, caressing, coaxing, and finally demanding the response she had willingly given.

Trembling, engulfed by the fever that consumed him, she had stopped trying to push him away. Instead her arms had crept round him and, awed by the quivering rigidity of his muscles and barely controlled strength, she clung to him, intoxicated by his driving need. Straining towards him, she was nervous, yet not afraid, and gloried in her ability to rouse him so.

As his mouth had ravaged hers with a fervour that made her head swim and her body languorous with wave upon wave of throbbing warmth, she had been vaguely aware of his hand between them. Moments later her jacket and shirt were pushed aside and, with a shuddering groan, Adam had buried his face against the soft mound of her breast.

Then it had happened. As she clasped his dark head to her, her clamouring heartbeat matching his hot breath on her skin, he had suddenly torn himself free and, scrambling to his feet, had stumbled to the window, supporting himself with outstretched arms against the frame, his head bent, shoulders heaving as he sucked in air in great gasps.

Stunned, feeling as though part of herself had been torn away, she had lain sprawled on the rug until the cold air on her bare skin had shocked her into movement.

Jerking upright, she had fumbled her shirt and jacket around her, refastening buttons with shaking fingers, unable to believe what had almost happened, what certainly *would* have happened had Adam not stopped.

Shelley closed her eyes, stricken with mortification and bewilderment. Adam had been the one to call a halt, not her. For all her independence, her so-called hatred of him, he could have made love to her on the drawing-room floor of his house, and she would not have stopped him. Not because she *couldn't,* but because she would not have wanted to.

She felt slightly sick. What was wrong with her? She had run away from him once, turning her back on everything known and familiar, sustained only by a belief in herself and a capacity for hard work. He was about to close her business down. Because of him her friends were deserting her, and yet only a few moments ago she had been in his arms, experiencing a pleasure she had never known.

'I'll take you home,' Adam had said in a voice she scarcely recognised, and as he turned from the window she saw, despite the cold March air, beads of sweat like blisters on his forehead.

She had knelt to clear up the remains of the meal, but he had curtly ordered her to leave it. He would be returning after he dropped her off.

Once more the journey had been made in silence. This time there was no music. Adam had driven the car hard and fast, his mouth set grimly, his hands gripping the steering wheel as if he wanted to tear it apart.

Her own thoughts had been chaotic, flying in all directions like sparks from a bonfire. Yet the silence said more than words. It was an acknowledgement that they both needed space and time. It also made very plain that things were by no means finished between them.

Awareness of this filled Shelley with an uneasy mixture of dread and relief. Sooner or later she would have to face the complexities and contradictions within herself. But the confrontation could be put off until she felt more capable of dealing with the results.

The brief glance they exchanged as Adam let her out at the top of the slip revealed his own conflict. They did not say goodbye. She closed the door quietly and stood back as he gunned the engine and roared off down the quiet street.

Keeping herself busy for the rest of the day, she had tried not to think, not to remember how it felt to be in his arms with the weight of his body on hers.

On her knees in front of the fire as she shovelled coal into the glowing embers and brushed the hearth, Shelley realised with a shock that even during their engagement there had never been the same urgency, the same hunger as there had been that afternoon.

She recalled Adam's tightly drawn expression, the nerve jumping at the angle of his jaw and the sweat standing out on his forehead. Thank God *he* had possessed the necessary strength, for she knew she could not have summoned the will to stop him.

Dropping the brush on the hearth, Shelley covered her flushed and burning face with her hands, rocking to and fro in a confusion of misery almost too deep to bear. It didn't make sense! He was responsible for the greatest unhappiness she had ever known, yet this afternoon she would have given herself to him and gloried in his lovemaking.

There had to be something wrong with her. Was she so desperate for a man that she could ignore all the pain Adam had caused her simply to satisfy a physical need?

No, that wasn't true. It couldn't be, for she had had plenty of opportunities to go out with other men. Word of her arrival in the town—a young, pretty artist with no apparent ties and something of an air of mystery—had rippled along the grapevine with surprising speed and Shelley had been startled by the number of men, young and not so young, who had hovered outside the Gallery during the lunch hour or just as she was clearing up.

Mostly they had been unattached, but a few, after passing the time of day and admiring her work, had hinted at wives who didn't understand them, and at her own need for masculine company and protection. Managing to control her irritation at this arrogant display of male ego, she made it clear she was not available.

One man had been very persistent, claiming to be the producer of a small independent film company. He had told her he could get her into movies if she was interested. Shelley had laughed, thinking such a line too ridiculous and corny even to be angry at.

Only much later had she learned he had been genuine. But the knowledge had not caused her any regrets.

Only Gary, whom she instinctively realised posed no threat, had been allowed past the protective barrier she had erected against being hurt again to become her closest friend. But even he, though wholly male, had never been permitted more than brief, brotherly kisses.

Fortunately, though occasionally disappointed, he seemed to accept the limit on the physical aspect of their relationship. He never asked questions, but by carefully dropped remarks let her know he guessed she had been badly hurt, and that he would not pressure her.

Whether he had other, more obliging girlfriends, Shelley neither knew nor cared. She was content and grateful for what they shared and did not concern herself with matters she considered none of her business.

But this new insight left her in a deeper quandary than ever, for it signified that her need was not simply for any man, but for one in particular, Adam Trelawney. Her first love. The man who had turned his back on her and buried himself in work rather than reveal his feelings. A man incapable of sharing himself. Any relationship with such a man was doomed from the start.

Perhaps she *had* been wrong. Her immediate assumption had been that he had come to Cornwall to seek her out, to avenge himself. But maybe he had been as surprised and shaken as she when their paths crossed. Had he not said she had wasted time and energy covering her tracks, for he had had no intention of trying to find her? But surely pride would have made him say that, anyway.

If his purchase of the house across the water really was a coincidence and nothing to do with the fact that she was living and working in the town, why were they meeting so frequently?

With biting sarcasm he had mocked her presumption that there was a personal motive behind his reappearance in her life, and he had had a legitimate reason for every contact with her.

So why had he kissed her? Why had he begun to make love to her only to tear himself away at the last moment?

A yawning chasm opened up inside Shelley. Had that too been just another point he wanted to prove? That despite time, distance and their mutual antipathy, his hold over her was stronger than ever?

Shivering with a chill that touched her heart, Shelley rose stiffly from the window seat, turning her back on the lemon and primrose sunrise.

She was at the Gallery just after eight and, as she opened the door and switched on the lights, she almost trod on an envelope. It contained a key and a scribbled note from Sue wishing her all the best from John and herself.

Absently, Shelley dropped her bag on her padded stool and, fingering the key, gazed at the area where, only a few days ago, John had been working. His vast table had been strewn with strips of moulding, sheets of board, a hammer, boxes of tacks, tubes of glue, clamps, jars of brushes, tubes of paint and rags. His easel had stood beside the window and a stack of canvases in various stages of preparation had been propped against the wall. The two screens that bounded his work area had been covered with his paintings, framed and ready for sale. Now they were bare. Everything had gone.

Sue's corner was the same. The boxes of rainbow-hued silk and chiffon, the coils of fine wire covered in green plastic, trays of multi-coloured thread, the tiny oval black velvet cushion which, bristling with needles, resembled a porcupine, had all disappeared. As had the many different pairs of scissors and pliers, and the vases full of finished blooms.

Shelley looked around. Kath's spinning-wheel stood in its usual place. She had a smaller, folding one she took to shows. But soon all her things would be going as well. Already the atmosphere was different. She was here on borrowed time. Drawing in a deep, shaky breath, Shelley dropped the key in her bag and went to take off her coat.

She worked steadily, shutting her mind to everything but the flame and the glass. She made four more snowdrops. Then, obeying an impulse, took a strip of black shiny glass and began to fashion the slender, flowing shape of a prowling cat.

She was so absorbed she didn't see Gary come in, and started when, leaning over the screen, he whistled in admiration.

'That's new, isn't it? I haven't seen you do one of those before. What is it? I mean,' he added quickly, 'I can see it's a cat. But that's not the sort you'd find lying on a rug in front of the living-room fire.'

Shelley blinked and wriggled her shoulders, easing the strain of concentration. 'It's a black leopard.' She stared at the sleek, sinuous shape gripped in the tweezers. 'Sometimes called a panther.'

Gary's eyebrows climbed. 'Not your usual thing, is it?'

Shelley shrugged. 'I'm broadening my scope.'

Gary looked at it again. 'It's one of the best things you've ever done, Shell,' he said slowly. 'Do you know who it reminds me of?'

'What do you mean, *who*?' she laughed. 'It's an animal, not a person.' But as she gazed at the gleaming black cat her smile faded and she recognised the unconscious thought which had prompted the sculpture.

With its head down, ears flattened, body and tail low to the ground, it was the ultimate predator, frozen in the instant of sighting its prey.

Her throat dried and she had to swallow before she could speak. 'I—I'm going to do an otter and a couple of seals, as well.'

Gary's eyes were fixed on the panther. 'Cartoon stuff compared with this.'

Shelley shrugged, pretending a casualness she did not feel, and set the panther on the display shelf with unsteady fingers. 'The customers like them, and they pay the wages. Speaking of which, don't you have work to do?'

'I'm going to form a union,' Gary threatened as he stalked off to his machine, 'to protect admiring leathercraft workers from bossy glass sculptresses.'

'Are you expecting many applicants?' Shelley called over her shoulder.

'Well, there's me,' he retorted. 'I'm fast becoming an endangered species.'

They did not have a single customer all morning.

'Anyone would think we'd closed down already,' Gary groaned. 'I'm off to drown my sorrows. You coming for a drink? I'll treat you to a pasty.'

Shelley shook her head. 'I brought a flask and sandwiches. I'll mind the shop while you go.'

'It doesn't look as if you'll be rushed off your feet,' Gary said gloomily.

'Monday is usually quiet,' Shelley said, trying to calm her own fears as well as his.

But Tuesday was no better, and nor was Wednesday, though by Wednesday evening Shelley had managed to replenish her display shelves and stock cabinet, and make up for the time lost during her illness and holiday.

She worked with steady determination, arriving early and not leaving before six. Flowers, birds and animals took shape and grew in the flame, their jewel colours glowing on the mirrored shelves.

She responded to Gary's banter and smiled at his terrible jokes. But as the days passed with no word or

sign from Adam, instead of relaxing and breathing a
sigh of relief, Shelley felt herself growing more and
more tense.

Where was he? What was he doing? Why had he
not been in touch? Even as the questions formed in
her mind, she mocked herself bitterly.

Wasn't this exactly what she had wanted? For him
to get out of her life and leave her in peace? But this
wasn't peace. This gnawing uncertainty was a form of
torture. Was this absence permanent or only tempo-
rary? Why, after dogging her footsteps for days, had
he suddenly dropped out of sight? Was it something
to do with what had happened at the house? But what
had happened? Not enough, or too much? Did he
despise her, assuming she responded like that to
anyone? Did it matter what he thought?

Shelley paused in the act of brushing her hair,
staring into her dressing-table mirror. 'No!' she
muttered fiercely at her reflection. 'Damn him! Let
him think what he likes.' She flung down the brush
and, picking up her cashmere coat from the bed, went
downstairs.

She wished she were not going out, but a promise
was a promise. And even as she locked her front door
and walked up the slip, she was telling herself it was
really just what she needed. Being at home, alone with
her thoughts, was driving her mad. She had spring-
cleaned the cottage, tidied drawers and cupboards,
and washed all the curtains. She had cleaned the oven,
a job she loathed, until it positively sparkled, and
chopped enough firewood to last until autumn. Every
moment of the past three days had been crammed
with activity.

Yet despite the warm bath and milky drink each
night, still she could not sleep properly. Exhausted,
she would go out like a light the instant her head hit
the pillow, only to wake two hours later, her thoughts
racing like a runaway train. From then on, despite

every effort of will, she was plagued by images of
Adam. Adam smiling and relaxed, his arm around her
waist, pointing to boats sailing in the bay as the sun
sparkled on the water and a breeze ruffled their hair.
Adam, with cruel mouth and cold eyes making some
scathing remark she could never catch. Adam, his face
clouded with passion, his arms enfolding her as ripples
of desire hardened the body pressing hers down on to
the tartan rug.

She would toss and turn until, unable to stand the
torment of body and mind, she would creep downstairs
and, stirring up the embers of the fire, drink cups of
tea or coffee until dawn broke and it was time to dress
and face the day.

Gary noticed her preoccupation and the violet
shadows under her eyes and made his own interpre-
tation of the cause.

'Look, don't worry about it, Shell,' he said. 'We'll
find another place soon. Every estate agent in town is
on the look-out. Something will turn up, you'll see.'

She stared at him blankly.

'Don't you trust me?' he teased.

She smiled wearily. 'Of course I do.'

'Then stop fretting and leave it all to your Uncle
Gary! Believe me, Shell, in a month's time you'll be
looking back on this and wondering what the fuss was
about.'

'I hope so,' she had said, wanting desperately to
believe him even though they were talking about
different things.

She walked up the path, bordered on each side by
a narrow strip of lawn with a flowerbed in the centre.
A few dead leaves still clung to the straggly rose-
bushes around which weeds were sprouting.

She knocked on the door and running feet thumped
along the passage. The door was flung open by a
bright-eyed boy of twelve wearing brand-new jeans
and a red lumberjack-style shirt. His face was scrubbed

and shiny and his hair was slicked down with water.
'It's her!' the boy yelled over his shoulder.

'Hello, David,' Shelley smiled. 'You look smart.'

'Didn't want to,' he grumbled, 'but Mum made me
'cos you was coming.' Shelley's heart sank. Then, his
face alight with curiosity, David demanded, 'Is your
Dad really famous like Gary said?'

Like lead weights, Shelley's already precarious spirits
plummeted and she mentally braced herself for the
evening ahead. 'Sort of,' she allowed casually.

'You'd better come in.' He stood back and Shelley
forced herself over the doorstep. 'Hey, fancy you being
rich. You never let on.' He sounded both awed and
accusing.

'I'm not,' Shelley replied at once, trying to keep her
smile in place.

The boy frowned. 'Giddon, you must be if your
Dad's a sir and owns a bank. I bet you could buy a
speed boat and a flash sports car and a video and——'

'Lay off, David,' Gary said from behind him. 'It's
none of your business.' He aimed a light-hearted blow
which the boy avoided with an ease born of long
practise. 'Hi, Shell, come on in. 'Scuse the brat. Twelve
year olds are hell.'

She smiled dutifully, noticing how keyed-up he
seemed as he moved from one foot to the other, first
scratching his ear, then rubbing the back of his neck.
He didn't seem to know what to do with his hands.

She was surprised to see him wearing a tie, and he
had changed his usual cords for a pair of smartly
pressed, dark brown trousers and a lemon V-necked
sweater. His shoes were polished and his damp hair
was ridged with comb marks.

Shelley handed him her coat and watched him hang
it on one of the row of four pegs at the bottom of the
stairs. 'I wish you hadn't told them, Gary.'

He grinned at her but his eyes were wary. He
shrugged, sliding an oddly tentative arm around her

shoulders, and the powerful scent of his aftershave
caught in her throat.

It was different, all wrong somehow. The easy
banter had been replaced by self-consciousness and an
artificial joviality, but why?

'It just slipped out. Anyway, it's not a secret any
more, is it?'

'No,' she agreed, 'but it's not something I want to
talk about, either.'

He squeezed her shoulders. 'Relax. I don't know
what you're so bothered about. It doesn't make the
slightest difference to me.'

'Oh no?' Shelley challenged softly. 'What about
your parents?'

He shrugged again, his eyes sliding away from hers.
'You can't blame them if——'

'I'm not *blaming* them for anything,' Shelley interrupted. 'I just wish you hadn't said anything.' She
shook her head hopelessly. 'Everything's different now.'

His hand was damp as he clasped her fingers.
'You're still the same lovely girl, and I——' He broke
off. 'You look smashing. That green really suits you.'

Shelley glanced down at her broad-belted dress of
soft wool. Her tan high heels and handbag matched
her coat. 'Thank you.' She smiled briefly, accepting
the compliment, too concerned with what was to come
to wonder what he had been going to say before he
changed his mind.

Mrs Hall had clearly gone to a lot of trouble over
the meal. A joint of roast pork, the crackling done to
a crisp, golden brown, was served with roast potatoes,
carrots, cabbage, apple sauce and gravy, and followed
by apple crumble and clotted cream.

But what little appetite Shelley had was spoiled by
probing questions from David and his mother's
constant apologies which Shelley found impossible to
brush aside without sounding patronising.

Tracey, Gary's sixteen-year-old sister, clearly

resented all the fuss and made several snappy comments about rich outsiders taking jobs from local people. Shelley sympathised with her point of view and said so. But Gary leapt to her defence and asked if Tracey knew anyone who could do Shelley's job, which, he pointed out acidly, was highly specialised and the result of several years' hard study and training.

Shelley could have screamed. She knew he meant well, but she had not needed defending. By choosing not to take Tracey's remarks personally she had defused the situation—until Gary had jumped in with both feet. She realised he was trying to expunge his own guilt at having caused the strained atmosphere by revealing her background, but it didn't help much.

'I know this isn't what you're used to,' Mrs Hall said several times, her rosy face puckered with concern as her eyes darted round the room, lighting with apparent unease on the clean but faded loose covers, the worn carpet, and the mantelshelf above the Rayburn crammed with ornaments, letters, a pipe and tobacco pouch, two boxes of matches and a model racing car.

'No easy job bringing up a family these days,' Gary's father put in. 'What with the junk they do put on the telly, and they there pop groups, and wages down 'ere being what they are.'

'It must be a problem,' Shelley agreed and Tracey snorted, raising her eyes to the ceiling, then with an exaggerated 'Excuse me' flounced out.

Mrs Hall smiled nervously. 'She do think we're old-fashioned.'

'Maybe we are, but we've never owed no one, not a penny.' Mr Hall said it proudly, reaching for his pipe and cleaning it into a large ashtray. 'There's not many can say that.'

Shelley nodded, not sure what was expected of her. Gary's parents had always treated her with a mixture of deference and curiosity, but tonight the deference had noticeably increased, yet was spiked with aggression.

'Always bin in work, too,' he affirmed. 'Never drawn the dole, not 'ad nothing off the State. We might not 'ave much, but what we got was earned fair and square, no 'and-outs.'

'You have a lot to be proud of, Mr Hall,' Shelley said, meaning every word, 'and Gary seems set to follow your example.'

'Oh yes,' Mrs Hall beamed. 'Done well for 'isself, Gary 'ave. Made 'is Dad and me some pleased. Not afraid of 'ard work, not like some round 'ere. Got 'is own business and a bit put by. Make a fine 'usband 'e will.'

'*Mum,*' Gary muttered, blushing scarlet and grinning sheepishly as he caught Shelley's eye.

'I'm sure he will, Mrs Hall,' Shelley agreed, enjoying Gary's discomfort after her own ordeal. 'In fact, I'm surprised there isn't a queue.'

'Aw, get on,' Mrs Hall simpered, 'since you come down 'ere 'e 'aven't looked at no one else. 'E's no flirt, not like some. A good-living boy, Gary is.'

Shelley smiled and nodded. As both parents watched her, obviously expecting some comment she added, 'Gary's friendship has meant a great deal to me, Mrs Hall.'

The older couple exchanged a knowing glance. 'Well, we never thought 'e'd bring 'ome a girl like you, did us, dear?' Mrs Hall looked at her husband for confirmation and he nodded sagely over his pipe. 'But I tell 'ee this, 'e might not 'ave the kind of money you're used to, but money isn't everything, and there's not a kinder boy living than Gary.'

Shelley nodded, completely lost for words. A gap had opened up between the Halls and herself that had not existed, or at least had not been noticeable, before they learned the truth about her background. Despite her own and Gary's efforts to steer the conversation

on to less controversial topics, Mrs Hall had returned
again and again, like iron filings to a magnet, to
apologise for things which none of them had given a
thought to in the past. Shelley was saddened, and felt
unaccountably lonely. When she offered to help with
the dishes, Mrs Hall looked horrified and would not
hear of it.

'David and Tracey'll be back down to watch
something on the telly in a bit o' while, so why don't
you two go in the front room? Get on now, I can
manage. I 'aven't fergotten what 'tis like when you're
courting.' She smiled coyly and shooed them out into
the passage.

As the door closed, Shelley hesitated, then half
turned, rubbing her forehead with the tips of her
fingers. 'Gary, if you don't mind, I'd rather go home.
I'm awfully tired.'

'You've hated every minute of it, haven't you?' he
said miserably.

'Of course not,' Shelley protested, forcing convic-
tion into the lie. 'It was a lovely meal.' Unbidden, the
memory of the evening she had spent with Adam at
the Waterfront restaurant flashed through her mind.
Adam. He was responsible for tonight's débâcle. If he
had not compelled her to reveal the truth of her
background to the others at the Gallery—she sighed.
It was too late for regrets and recriminations. 'Your
parents are nice people, Gary. They love you and are
proud of you.'

He held her coat while she slipped her arms in, then
picked up his anorak and pushed open the living-
room door.

'I'm taking Shelley home,' he shouted above the
noise of the television set. His mother came hurrying
out of the kitchen, wiping her hands on a tea-towel,
her round face creased with concern.

'I was just going to make a cup of tea. You can
stay and have that, can't you?'

Shelley stretched her mouth into a passable imitation of a smile. 'Honestly, Mrs Hall, I couldn't manage another thing. I really enjoyed the meal. It's just that, well, what with one thing and another, I'm rather tired.'

Gary's mother surveyed her with a critical eyes, her motherly instincts overriding her deference. 'You do need looking after and feeding up a bit. 'T wouldn' take no more than a breath of wind to blow 'ee away.'

Shelley grinned wearily. 'Mrs Hall, if you had your way I'd look like a suet dumpling within a week. I promise you, I do take care of myself but, like Gary, I also have a business to run.'

'Better ef you 'ad a 'usband to take care of 'ee, and a baby or two,' the older woman muttered.

'Mum!' Gary warned, but she ignored him, patting Shelley's arm.

'Must be some worry for 'ee, finding another place an' all. I 'ope it do work out all right, dear. 'Twas lovely seeing 'ee. You come again mind, soon as you like.'

'Thank you.' Shelley felt the prickle of tears at the woman's transparent kindness. If only her mother—she cut the thought off and walked quickly out on to the path.

Gary was unusually quiet as they walked down the road towards the harbour and Shelley's cottage. The street lamps cast pools of orange light which made the shadows even darker. The night air was cold and damp and very still. Their footsteps were loud on the flagged pavement.

'Shell,' Gary began, his voice taut, 'she could be right.'

'Who? About what?' Involved with her own thoughts, Shelley gazed unseeingly at the pavement as she walked, her bag tucked under her arm, her hands deep in the pockets of her coat.

'Mum. You need looking after.'

There was no humour in her brief smile. 'I'm really quite capable, Gary.'

'Yes, I know, but you don't *have* to do it all alone.'

'What do you suggest? A couple of servants? My income doesn't stretch——'

'No,' he interrupted, an audible tremor in his voice, 'like she said—a husband. Me.'

Shelley's head jerked round. The blood drained from her face as her mouth fell open in total astonishment. They faced one another, their faces ghostly in the artificial light.

'I hadn't planned—I mean, I was going to ask you but—look, what about it, Shell? I think the world of you. I know I haven't got a lot to offer, not in the way of a house or car, but you'd never want for the important things.' He watched her intently, his own hands deep in his trouser pockets.

'I—I—Gary, I don't know what to say,' Shelley stammered. Suddenly his parents' probing and hints all began to fall into place. 'You've discussed this with your family?'

He ground a weed growing up between two flagstones to pulp with the toe of his shoe. 'Not discussed, no. But they might have guessed. I—well, I do talk about you a lot.'

'I wish you hadn't told them about me,' she said softly.

'I had to, didn't I?' He shrugged awkwardly. 'Anyway, it's nothing to be ashamed of.'

'I'm not ashamed,' Shelley said quickly. 'It's just that I've cut all ties with my past and I see no point in raking it all up again.'

'Not *all* ties, Shell,' he corrected, his expression serious. 'But I could help you do that. You've been hurt enough. I don't want to see it happen again.'

The shadow of Adam loomed between them. Gary's obvious sincerity touched Shelley deeply. For an instant she was tempted. Gary was gentle and kind. There

was nothing remotely threatening about him. He would
adore her, give her everything he had. *And it would
never be enough.*

There was no way to soften the rejection, or to
make the truth more palatable, for she had to tell him
the truth, she owed him that.

'Your friendship has always been very special to
me, Gary.' As he recognised the implication in her
words excitement and hope faded from his face, leaving
it dull and drawn. 'And that's the way I've always
thought of you, as a dear and close friend.'

'But nothing more,' he said flatly.

She shook her head.

'It's Trelawney, isn't it?' he blurted. 'John was right,
there is still something between you. What's the matter
with you, Shell? Are you blind? He's hard and cruel.
He doesn't give a damn for anyone, can't you see
that?'

'Gary, you're making it sound as though my only
choice is between you and Adam. There are other men
in the world.' She was trying to deflect him and they
both knew it. His face was tight and full of hurt.

'I said once before that I couldn't compete with
Trelawney and you said I didn't have to. But that's
what it comes down to in the end. Everything changed
when he turned up. I think maybe John and Sue and
Kath have done the right thing, after all.'

'Gary, don't, please——'

'It's better if we forget about working together. I'll
find somewhere on my own.'

'Is this what you call friendship?' Shelley asked
quietly. 'Walking away when I need you most?'

His laugh was high-pitched, strangled. 'You've never
needed me. I've been useful, a comfort, like a hot-
water bottle or old slippers. Oh, you've been glad of
my company, but there's always been a barrier between
us. You kept it there. I thought if I was patient
enough, if I gave you time, didn't push, then maybe

you would——' He broke off. 'Ah, what the hell!'

'Gary, don't leave,' Shelley pleaded, her voice low, desperate. He was all she had left.

'What is there to stay for?' he shot back. 'Nothing's going to change, is it?'

'You're rushing me——' she began.

'Don't give me that,' he responded with uncharacteristic vehemence. 'I've never pressured you and you know it. Perhaps if I had——' He shrugged, the quick movement angry and full of frustration. He gave her a hard look. 'Will you marry me?'

She raised her head. Her skin felt like a mask stretched across her cheekbones. An iron band of tension tightened around her skull. 'Gary——'

'An answer, Shelley, yes or no.'

'I can't,' she whispered.

'Then it's no good.' His voice held a mixture of resignation and sadness. 'I'll get a place by myself, someone's bound to have a garage or workshop I can use.' For an instant, his vulnerability showed through. 'I can't face seeing the two of you together.' Then his expression hardened. 'He's hurt you once, Shell, and he'll do it again. But this time I won't be around to pick up the pieces.'

The impulse to lash back was almost irresistible, but Shelley managed to control it, realising that his pride as well as his feelings had been badly hurt.

With a calmness that was barely skin-deep she met his gaze. 'It's your decision, Gary. Three years is a long time and you have been more help to me than you'll ever know. But I'm not the right person for you. You'll meet other girls.' He snorted and turned his head away. 'Yes, you will,' she insisted, 'and you'll ask one of them to marry you, and she will make you far happier than I ever could. You deserve the best. You've been the dearest friend anyone could have wished for.' Her voice trembled and she swallowed, her eyes hot with unshed tears. So many partings—so much ended.

He looked anguished. 'Shell, I——' But she shook her head, gripping his arm.

'It's all been said. Will you be at the Gallery tomorrow?'

He shrugged, not answering. 'Come on.' His voice was dull. 'I'll take you home.'

She shook her head again, aware of a throbbing ache in her temples. 'I—I'd rather go alone.'

He hunched his shoulders, but a look of relief stole across his features. 'Sure you'll be all right?'

'Of course I will.' She tried to smile. 'It's only a spit away.'

He studied his shoes, shamefaced yet anxious to get away. 'Think I'll go and have a drink then. 'Night, Shell.'

Suddenly he looked very young. 'Goodnight, Gary.' And goodbye. He was right. There was no going back. The next time they met, barriers would be firmly in place.

She crossed the town centre and walked quickly down the slip to the quay. In Elsie's living-room the light glowed dimly through the closed curtains, and the sound of voices and laughter floated out as Elsie watched a comedy show on TV.

Next door, at Frank and Doreen's, the upstairs lights were on as well. In the unusually still air she heard Frank call up to ask his wife if she wanted a cup of tea.

Shelley let herself into her own cottage, closing the door quietly. With the precision of a surgeon, Adam had separated her from all the people who over the last three years had been her friends. She was totally alone again. This time the hurt was much worse.

CHAPTER SEVEN

THE SLEEVES of Elsie's old grey cardigan were pushed up almost to her elbows. Her hands looked purplish-red in the cold air as she shook out a small rug a few paces from her open front door

Beneath the cardigan, which she never buttoned, over a plain blouse, she wore a sleeveless wrap-around cotton overall, so old and faded the pattern of tiny blue flowers was barely discernible. Thick stockings encased what could be seen of her legs beneath her favourite brown tweed skirt, and her feet were pushed into fawn carpet slippers with buttons and pom-poms on the front.

'You 'aven't left nothing out in the back yard, 'ave'ee, my 'andsome?'

Shelley looked up from locking her front door. 'No, why?'

'Be raining by lunchtime,' Elsie announced.

Shelley tilted her head, observing the thick blanket of low grey cloud. A sharp-edged breeze was blowing straight up the river, creaming the tops off lumpy waves the colour of slate. The tide was two hours into the ebb, but the water, held in the river by the wind, still slapped midway up the quay wall.

'The forecast wasn't too bad,' Shelly said hopefully. 'They promised sunny periods later this morning,' Even as she spoke, a ray of pale, watery sunlight forced its way through a break in the cloud. They both looked towards it, but the gap closed again, shutting off the beam, and the greyness seemed even more sombre.

'False promises, my bird.' Elsie was derisive and the words echoed in Shelley's head. 'They never get it right for down 'ere. I tellee there's a nasty bit o' weather coming. None o' the fishermen've gone this morning. It don't look up to much in 'ere, but 't will be ten times worse out there.' She gestured towards the harbour month. 'Bad wind for us, the south-easter is.'

Shelley shivered and turned up the collar of her coral-coloured padded jacket. 'I hope you're wrong, Elsie.' Bad weather meant no customers and it had already been a disastrous week from that point of view. In fact, taken all round it had been one of the worst weeks she had ever known.

The old woman shuffled back to her front door. 'Wish I was, my 'andsome.' But her tone said she knew she wasn't. ' 'Ere, do 'ee know where Mr Trelawney is to? Only 'e's s'posed to be sending this 'ere builder to do my wall, but 'e never said what day.' Shelley shook her head, not trusting herself to speak. 'You know 'e bought the big 'ouse?' Elsie pointed across the river, but did not wait for a reply. 'Well, Rosie Thomas was telling me she 'eard 'e's doing some 'andsome job over there. Spending thousands 'e is. Be some beautiful place when e've finished. 'E've put in a 'andsome new kitchen, and that there central 'eating. And 'e got one o' they fizzy baths. Great round thing it is.' She looked at Shelley expectantly, waiting for her reaction to this news.

'Jacuzzi,' Shelley murmured, seeing it clearly and hearing Adam's deep voice, vibrant with laughter and irony, inviting her to try it. 'Double bathing can be fun,' he had said. Goose-flesh erupted on her arms.

'What?' Elsie's gaze was intent.

'That's what those fizzy baths are called, jacuzzis,' she explained quickly.

'Ah!' Elsie nodded. 'Well, seems to me the only thing 'e do need now is a wife.' She tucked her chin in, continuing archly, 'And there's more than a few out to catch un, so I've 'eard.' Her voice sharpened. ''Ere, you all right, my bird? You aren't looking all that special.'

How did Elsie know that? Where had she heard it? Shelley swallowed hard. What was it to her if Adam Trelawney had a whole fleet of girlfriends? 'I'm fine,' her voice was over-bright. Did he kiss them the same way he had kissed her? 'A bit tired, that's all.' Was that why she hadn't seen him since Sunday, three of the longest days in her life? Was he looking for someone more experienced, more sophisticated? Was he really planning to marry? Or was that just Elsie's wishful thinking? There was no way she could ask without signalling her interest, on which Elsie would pounce like a hawk.

'I knew you wasn't sleeping proper,' Elsie frowned 'I've 'eard 'ee moving about in the night. When you get my age you don't need so much sleep. But a young maid like you, working 'ard, it's no good for 'ee.' She paused. 'Wha's the matter, my bird?' There was curiosity in her voice, but there was also kindness and that was nearly Shelley's undoing. She ached to put her head on Elsie's ample bosom and let all her misery pour out. Blinking rapidly to dispel the welling tears, she kept her head down, pretending to search for something in her bag.

'Nothing. It's just—the move and everything.' She gave a helpless shrug.

'You 'aven't found anywhere else then?'

Head bent, Shelley made a brief negative movement.

''Ow don't 'ee ask Mr Trelawney?' Elsie suggested. ''E'd soon find 'ee somewhere.'

'I wouldn't ask him if——' Shelley exploded and stopped abruptly, drawing in a shuddering breath as she looked up to meet Elsie's shrewd gaze. 'There's still a few days before I have to move out.' Her voice wobbled she cleared her throat. 'Plenty of time.'

' 'Ad a quarrel, 'ave 'ee?' Elsie's voice was full of sympathy.

Shelley buried her face in her hands and her shoulders heaved as she shook her head. They hadn't quarrelled, had they? He had been holding her, kissing her as though—as though—then suddenly he wasn't holding her any more. She was alone, more alone than she had ever been in her life, and he had let her out of the car and driven away and she hadn't seen him since. *Why had she let it happen?* She hated herself and she hated him.

Elsie enfolded her in comforting arms and patted Shelley's back as though she was a child. 'All too much, is it, my bird? Don't 'ee fret now. 'Twill all come all right in the end. It always do. Do 'ee wanna talk about it?'

Shelley gulped and sniffed as she shook her head, fumbling in her pockets for a tissue. 'I'm not crying over Adam Trelawney,' she said, wiping her eyes and blowing her nose, trying to convince herself. 'I wouldn't waste my tears. It's—it's the Gallery. Now Gary is leaving as well.'

'What about it?' Elsie demanded with spirit. 'You started out on your own, didn'ee? 'S nothing to get in such a tizz about. Look, if it do come to the worst, you can work in your own front room or your kitchen, and sell your stuff in Kessell's. The best shop in town fer china and glass, that is. Young Will do run the place now, I b'lieve, but 'is father is my second cousin. I'm going up the town in a bit o' while. I'll talk to un, see if 'e'll let 'ee 'ave that there stand in the small window. The round one down the bottom at the front. Your little figures would look 'andsome on that there green felt. An' you'd get good prices. No rubbish in that shop.' She gripped Shelley's arms, shaking her gently. 'Now, you just stop fretting and get off to work.'

Shelley opened her mouth, but before she could

protest, Elsie said firmly, 'I'm only going to ask what 'e *think* about it. If 'e's 'appy, you can go and talk to un yourself. You aren't bound to nothing. But I know un and you don't, so I can ask *unofficial* like, and no one need know nothing about it. All right?'

Shelley hugged her. 'Elsie,' she said softly, 'you really are a gem.' She kissed the old woman's lined cheek.

'Get on with 'ee now.' Elsie shooed her away. 'Put me all be'ind you 'ave.' But her scolding lacked bite. She paused outside her front door, watching Shelley's slim figure disappear round the corner and up the slip. The smile lingered in her sharp blue eyes as she pursed her lips thoughtfully.

Gary did not appear and, for once, Shelley found it almost impossible to concentrate. The rising wind rattled the windows and roared in gusts up the street. At lunchtime the fog-horn began sending out its mournful warning.

Clutching her coffee mug in both hands to warm them, Shelley crossed to the side of the Gallery overlooking the river and looked out. The outline of the headland opposite was blurred by murky drizzle. The house across the water looked almost ghostly. External work would be impossible in this weather. Perhaps the painters would all be working inside, restoring the moulded plaster ceilings to pristine white. What colours had Adam chosen for the walls? What about carpets, curtain fabrics and furniture? She turned her back to the window, trying to block out such treacherous imaginings, realising for the first time how much Adam's work must mean to him.

Everything had to be just right, no corners cut, no detail ignored. It had never occurred to her to doubt him when he claimed that the standards he was setting for the work on his own property were no different to those he insisted upon for all the buildings he restored.

She had always thought of his work as something

that came between them and kept them apart. Yet it need not have done so had she not been so wrapped up in her own career. She could have shared his interest.

There was more to Adam's demand for the highest possible standards than simply getting the top price for a property once it was restored. He *cared*. Why had she not recognised that before? The answer came like a slap in the face. Because she had been too immersed in herself and her own concerns. Why could she see that now, when it was too late?

Shelley ate her sandwiches with little appetite and tried desperately to keep her thoughts on the figures she had yet to do, planning method and technique, reviewing different poses and deciding on those most appealing.

By four, dusk had set in and the wind-driven drizzle hissed against the streaming windows. She had not seen a single customer all day. 'Right,' she announced to the empty room, 'that's it.'

She turned off the gas cylinders, switched out the lights and put on her jacket, wishing she had taken more notice of Elsie's eye for the weather and brought an umbrella. She sighed. It was that sort of day.

After her usual check to ensure everything was safe, she took a final look at the display. The panther crouched on the second of the stepped shelves. It drew the eye, its brooding presence overshadowing all the other figures. Gary had been right, it *was* one of the best things she had ever done. But its sinuous black shape, exuding latent power, diminished the rest of the display.

Leaning over, Shelley lifted it from the shelf and moved the other figures to fill the gap. She was startled at the difference. Despite the dusky gloom, the clear glass sparkled, the green and white of the snowdrops held a real promise of spring, and the opalised figures shimmered, their delicate pastel shades defying the wrath of wind and rain.

Wrapping the panther in tissue paper, Shelley put it carefully into her bag. Out of sight, out of mind? an inner voice taunted. With all her heart she wished it could be so.

Her shoulders hunched against the bitter cold and her hands pushed deep into her jacket pockets, Shelley battled her way home in the teeth of the gale. The drizzle came at her almost horizontally, forcing her to screw her eyes up against the fine, needle-sharp spray.

By the time she reached the slip her hair was dripping, water was running down her neck and her face was stiff with cold. Thanks to the padding in her jacket her top half was still dry except for the soggy collar of her shirt. But her trousers were dark with rain and clung coldly to her thighs, and her feet were wet.

As she rounded the corner on to the quay she gasped and her stomach contracted unpleasantly. The river was a frenzied maelstrom of white foam. Above the howl and shriek of the wind she could hear mooring ropes and chains snapping taut as boats, large and small, were tossed skyward, as if the wild water wished to shake itself free of them. Waves smashed against the quay with a noise like thunder, sending clouds of spume and spray high into the air. Shelley could feel the vibration through her feet.

Shouts reached her on the wind and on the next quay, where the oystermen usually landed their haul, she could make out a group of men, some with ropes, others with long staves and oars, working feverishly to stop a cabin cruiser, which had evidently broken loose, from being smashed to pieces against the stone wall. Several boats would be lost that night, she guessed. Some would sink on their moorings, overwhelmed by the breaking waves. Others would be torn free and pounded to matchwood on the rocks at the far side of the river. The shiver that racked her

was not entirely due to the cold. There was something
frightening about a storm of this ferocity.

Three sandbags were already in place outside Elsie's
front door. As Shelley raised her hand to knock and
check the old lady was all right, the door opened, and
Elsie staggered forward, her shoulders bowed beneath
the weight of another sandbag.

'Glad you're 'ome, my bird,' she panted, dropping
the bag alongside the others. 'You'd better start
bringing yours out.'

'Has there been a flood warning?' Shelley asked
quickly.

Elsie straightened up, wincing as she clutched at the
door jamb with one hand and pressed the other
against the small of her back. 'No.' She shook her
head. 'I've 'ad Duchy Radio on all afternoon, but that
silly man kept saying the wind's going round to the
south-west. Well, it 'asn't changed yet and 't will be a
bit late when we got a foot o' water in our living-
rooms, won't it? 'Tis a spring tide, see.'

Shelley saw at once. The extra high tides which
occurred twice a month just after the new and full
moon, usually lapped the top edge of the quay, and
had twice, in the three years she had occupied the
cottage, actually reached the front door. With a wind
of this velocity behind it, the tide would almost
certainly be a foot higher than expected.

'You get on in,' Elsie ordered. ' 'igh water's at
eight.'

'Bags of time,' Shelley said with a confidence she
was far from feeling, but she could not leave the old
woman to cope alone. 'I'll help you first.' Without
waiting for a reply, she stepped over the threshold
into the dark, overcrowded little room. 'Could you
put the light on, Elsie? That'll make things a bit
easier.'

Elsie shook her head. 'Can't, my bird. 'lectric's
gone. Lines are down, see. There's slates falling like

leaves up the main street. Dougie Martin 'ave lost 'is chimney. Mind you, it nearly went the last gale we 'ad, but 'e wouldn' spend no money to 'ave it done. Any'ow, 'e says the council men are 'aving some job with all the fallen trees,' she snorted. 'They won't be short of a bit o' firewood. I was going to get me lamps and all out, but I thought I'd better do the door first.'

'I'll see to the door,' Shelley said. 'You get the lamps. Have you got paraffin?'

' 'Course I 'ave,' Elsie retorted. 'But I only got one pair of 'ands.'

While she rummaged in her kitchen cupboard, then under the stairs, Shelley started carrying the sandbags in. Already wet from being stacked out in the yard, they were back-breakingly heavy. She wondered how Elsie had managed to move the four already in place.

The drizzle turned to hard, driving rain, which battered Shelley's unprotected head as she gripped each bag with stiff, cold fingers, hefted it into her arms then stumbled through the kitchen, down the step into the living-room and to the front door. She had to balance the bag on her bent leg as she opened the door, jam the bag into place so there were no gaps through which the water could trickle, while the rain hammered down and her hands froze, then shut the door quickly and repeat the process.

By the time she had built a barricade almost three feet high, Elsie had filled and lit two oil lamps and set them on her sideboard. Their mellow light gave the room a cosy atmosphere. A third lamp stood on the old wooden table in the kitchen.

'I hope that will be enough, there aren't any more.' Shelley's legs felt weak and trembly, and her hands ached. But at least she wasn't cold anymore. Her shirt stuck to her, warmly clammy with perspiration.

'Tha's 'andsome.' Elsie bobbed her head. 'Now, you drink this.' She thrust a mug of steaming, dark brown liquid into Shelley's wet, sandy hands.

The tea was so strong it made Shelley shudder, but it was hot and sweet, and she felt its reviving warmth curl in her stomach and creep along her limbs. She gulped it down, burning her tongue, horribly aware that time was passing, the tide was still rising and she hadn't even begun the protection of her own cottage.

'Elsie, I'll have to go.' She put the mug down. 'Will you be all right?'

'My dear life, what are 'ee on about?' Elsie tutted. ' 'Course I'll be all right. I'm going in the kitchen by the range. I got me radio and me knitting, and a bit o' supper in th'oven.'

Shelley couldn't help smiling. 'Elsie, you're a marvel.'

'I don't know about that,' the old woman shrugged, 'but when you done all you can, there's no sense worrying, that don't do no good.'

As Shelley picked up her shoulder-bag, someone knocked, a loud, urgent tattoo, making her jump. She pulled open the door.

For a moment she did not recognise the short, square figure of her other next-door neighbour, muffled as he was in oilskins and scarf, with a sou'wester pulled low over his face.

'Shelley, can 'ee come and give us a 'and a minute?' He was slow-spoken, his voice deep and gravelly. 'I won't keep 'ee long, but Doris is fretting something awful and with 'er 'eart, well——' He let the sentence tail off, gazing with a mixture of hope and desperation at Shelley, who clambered unsteadily over the barricade.

'She's not having one of her turns, is she, Frank?' Achingly tired, and soaked through, Shelley could not turn her back on this plea for help, but nor could she cope if Doris was really ill.

'No,' he said, 'nothing like that.'

' 'Course she isn't,' Elsie added with a loud sniff. 'Doris 'aven't got a 'eart, so there can't be nothing wrong with it.'

'Elsie!' Shelley gasped.

'Now, come on, Else,' Fred said with a mildness that surprised Shelley even more.

'Frank, you know as well as I do they *turns* is only to keep you on the hop. Making you pay, she is, boy.'

Shelley stared at Elsie who, in the tone of a teacher addressing a backward pupil, explained, 'Bit of a lad, Frank was, in th'old days. Broke a few 'earts 'e did. 'Ad a way with un, didn' 'ee, boy?' This was addressed with a fond smile to the muffled figure, who showed not a sign of embarrassment.

Gazing into Frank's earnest face with its red nose, heavy jowls and watery eyes, Shelley tried to imagine him being 'a bit of a lad', but the picture simply wouldn't come.

'No, she's all right in 'erself, like,' he reassured them both, 'but she's going on 'bout the sandbags, says I'll do me back in if I try lifting 'em on me own. But she won't 'elp, and I can't just let the water come in, can I? She'll be moaning 'bout the bleddy carpet then.'

'I tell 'ee what,' Elsie said to Shelley, 'you go an' 'elp Frank while I go in and get a fire going for 'ee.'

Shelley shook her head. 'No, Elsie. You could catch pneumonia out in this.'

'Well, 's not doing none of us no good just standing 'ere,' Elsie chided.

'No, and you're not built for hurdling,' Shelley pointed out, indicating the wall of sandbags. 'You get back inside. I'll give Frank a hand, and I'll get started on my own flood barrier.'

'Mind you bang on the wall when you're finished, so I know you're all right.' Elsie reminded her.

Shivering as she began to chill off, Shelley nodded and Elsie closed the door.

Waves started to break over the quay. Shelley fought down a surge of panic. 'Frank, you go and tell Doris I'm coming. I just want to drop my bag inside and light my Tilley lamp. I'll be right with you.'

He hurried on to his own cottage. Hunched against the hammering rain Shelley fumbled her key into the lock with numb fingers. Her jaws ached as she gritted her teeth to stop them chattering. She heard the thud and splash of running feet down the slip and the beam of a powerful torch shone in her eyes, making her screw up her face and blink as she tried to see who it was.

'What on earth are you doing out in this?' Adam demanded roughly.

Shelley's heart leapt into her throat and the shock made her feel dizzy. 'I—I'm trying to get in,' she retorted, her voice scarcely recognisable. *He had come back.*

'Here, let me.' He focused the torch on the door, snatching the keys from her awkward fingers. 'You're frozen!' He made it sound like something she ought to be ashamed of, and turned the torch on her again. The beam swept her from head to toe.

Without being aware of it, Shelley raised one arm as if to ward off a blow.

'God almighty, Rochelle!' Adam exploded. 'What the hell have you been doing? You must be soaked to the skin.'

Shelley's hand touched her hair, now straggling in rats' tails around her pinched face. 'In case you hadn't noticed, it's raining,' she remarked with heavy sarcasm. 'And I've been helping Elsie with her sandbags.' Her joy and relief at his arrival was swiftly turning to anger and resentment, irrationally aggravated by sudden awareness of her bedraggled and filthy appearance.

He opened the door and shoved her roughly inside.

'Don't close it,' she warned, slinging her bag on to the sofa, remembering an instant too late that the zip was still undone. Sure enough, as it hit the cushions everything fell out. Her purse bounced on to the floor, flew open, and coins jingled against the hearth. She closed her eyes momentarily, then ignored it. 'I promised Frank I'd give him a hand. He's got a bad back and——'

'You're going nowhere,' Adam grated, 'except into a hot bath.'

Despite her weariness, hot bitter anger welled up in Shelley, so violent it made her tremble. 'Keep your orders for the people you employ,' she spat. 'Frank's wife is an invalid and I gave my word. Where——' she managed to change it at the last minute, 'what are you doing here, anyway?'

'I came to help,' he snapped.

'You needn't have bothered,' she replied at once, on the verge of tears and not understanding why.

'No, I can see you're managing beautifully,' he said drily. 'Look, I heard some of the locals talking in the bar about——' he paused as Shelley strangled a bitter laugh, '—about the combination of wind and tide, and I thought you might need a hand.'

'It took you long enough,' she blurted. *Three long days without a word.*

'I didn't get back from London until almost six,' he replied tartly.

'London?' she repeated blankly. 'But——' She bit her tongue. How long? She could not, would not ask. But at least it explained why she had not seen him. Anxious that he should not think he had been missed, desperate to cling to the shreds of dignity and self-respect she had left, Shelley said quickly, 'You could have saved yourself the journey, we're used to managing on our own.'

'So I see,' his tone was paper-dry, but also suddenly milder. Suspicious of this change, Shelley wished she could see his expression, but he kept the torch pointed just to one side of her, not enough to dazzle, but sufficient to keep his own face in darkness while illuminating hers. 'But now you'll manage that bit more quickly.'

He thrust the torch into her hands so suddenly she almost dropped it.

'Find a candle or something . . . I presume you have got another source of light?'

'Yes.' Shelley bit the word off.

'And get a fire going. *I'll* go and help your neighbour.' He strode out, slamming the door and it was then she realised he was bare-headed and wore only a leather jerkin over his trousers. Pearl-grey, expensive and totally unsuitable.

Hurrying to the cupboard under the stairs, Shelley dragged out the box containing the Tilley lamp. Her hands were shaking so badly it took three attempts to strike the match. *He had come back, but for how long*? Once more her emotions were in turmoil.

The lamp hissed softly, its bright warmth infinitely welcome after the rain and wind and blackness. Shelley set it on the table by the stairs and went to light the fire, thankful that her sleeplessness had prompted her to lay it early that morning instead of waiting until she got home, as she usually did.

The contents of her bag lay scattered over the sofa and rug. The tissue-paper wrapping had slipped off the panther and, for a moment, Shelley stopped breathing. Was it broken? A brief examination showed no damage so, anxious to get on with protecting her own home against the encroaching tide, she set the panther on the shelf above the hearth, swept the rest of her things into her bag, and stumbled to her feet, clutching the arm of the sofa to ward off the slight giddiness provoked by the sudden movement.

She had managed to set five sandbags just outside the door and was reeling in through the kitchen with a sixth when Adam returned.

She didn't even know he was there until he tried to take the gritty weight from her arms. Instinctively, she resisted. The sandbag represented security, it would keep her cottage safe and the storm at bay. So much had been taken from her . . .

She looked up, startled at the sound of her name,
her eyes wide and blinking as conscious thought
replaced the automaton state into which she had sunk.

'It's all right,' he said gently.

Shelley looked past him to the open doorway. The
lamplight illuminated the curls of foam surging over
the quay. Sheeting rain blew in, soaking the carpet
and adding to the trail of wet footprints crossing to
the kitchen and back. 'The tide——' she croaked,
swaying.

'It's all right, Rochelle,' he repeated, and as his
words registered she tried to concentrate. What was
that in his gaze? His eyes were dark and glittering.
She turned her head away. Admiration from Adam
Trelawney was as likely as snow in the Sahara. A trick
of the light, that was all. 'I'll have all the bags in place
before it's any threat to the cottage, I promise. Have
you a couple of old towels we can pack against the
bottom of the door, just in case of the odd leak?'

Shelley nodded. 'Airing cupboard.' She pointed
vaguely upstairs.

'Throw them down to me,' he instructed. 'Then get
out of those wet clothes and into a hot shower. Right
now, Rochelle,' he added in a tone that warned her
not to argue. She didn't have the strength, anyway.

Leaving the Tilley on the table so Adam could see
what he was doing, Shelley lit her other small oil lamp
and climbed wearily up the stairs.

Too tired to move, she stood in the shower, face
upturned, eyes closed and let the water, still hot
despite the power cut, cascade over her, easing the
cold stiffness from her aching muscles. As she began
to relax, so the sick exhaustion drained away, leaving
her merely tired.

The bathroom door opened. Living alone, she never
locked it, and tonight she had been too weary and
confused for it to occur to her. She jumped as Adam's

voice enquired, 'Have you drowned?'

'No,' she spluttered and, shaking the water out of
her eyes and pushing her hair back, she peered round
the curtain. 'What do you want?' Fear clenched her
stomach in an icy fist. 'Is something wrong?'

'No, so far we're watertight.' He glanced at his
watch. 'Still an hour to go, though.'

Shelley let her breath out with a rush.

'I said, so far,' Adam warned. 'Rochelle, wouldn't
it be wiser for you and your neighbours to move out
until the danger is past?'

'You have to be joking!' Her smile was genuinely
amused. 'I made exactly the same suggestion during
my first winter here. I was put very firmly in my place,
and it was explained that they had lived on this quay
for forty years and the only way any of them would
leave it was feet first in a pine box, but I was free to
do as I liked.'

'Fair enough. And they're right. You don't have to
stay.' Adam leaned against the door post and folded
his arms. He had removed his jerkin. His curly hair
was seal-shiny, and water trickled down his face,
sparkling in the flickering lamplight, to drip off his
chin. His silver-grey roll-neck of fine wool clung wetly
to his chest and shoulders, and his pale grey trousers,
streaked with mud and sand, were dark with rain. But
it was the sight of his bare feet on the cork tiles that
jolted within Shelley a realisation of how this scene
would look to an outsider. Yet the impression of
casual intimacy, of a long-established relationship, was
utterly false, *wasn't it*? She was beginning to feel
horribly confused again.

'Of course I must stay,' she answered sharply. 'This
is my home. Anyway, there's no real danger, only
inconvenience. Besides,' she added, without thinking,
'how could I ever face them again if I ran away?'

'Doubtless you would convince them you had a
good reason,' Adam replied expressionlessly.

The flush of painful embarrassment made Shelley break out in a fine sweat. 'Do you mind if we continue the conversation later?' she asked with feigned coolness. 'I'd like to get out now.'

'Don't let me stop you.'

'Adam——'

He eased his tall frame upright, the top of his head grazing the surround. 'I came to tell you I've set a tray. Do you have a primus, or camping stove?'

'Yes, but——'

'Well, where is it?' he asked with exaggerated patience. 'I can't make us a hot drink without something on which to boil water.'

'In the cupboard under the stairs, left hand side, at the back. But you don't have to——'

'Tea or coffee?' he cut in.

'Tea, please.'

'Don't be long.' he went out, closing the door and Shelley heard his footsteps speeding down the stairs.

She remained under the shower for a few moments, partly in defiance, knowing it was a petty reaction, yet determined in some small way to make a stand. She was disturbed by the way he was able to simply take over without her being fully aware of what was happening until it was too late. There was something insidious about the effect he had on her, about her lack of will to fight, about his magnetic attraction.

Away from him she saw only too clearly the danger of her own personality being submerged by his, yet still missed him. But when they were together the battle lost its savour as she learned more about him and thus, in a roundabout way, more about herself.

She waited for the hot water to soothe away the goose-flesh that had erupted as she recalled Adam's eyes, hooded, gleaming with silent laughter and something else, something new and appraising, something she hadn't seen before.

Glowing from a vigorous towelling, dressed in an

old but comfy pair of cords and a lambswool sweater,
her feet warm in sheepskin moccasins, Shelley scooped
up her wet clothes and went downstairs. She had
brushed her still damp hair into a loose ponytail and
her fringe feathered softly across her forehead.

Adam was sitting forward in the armchair to the
left of the fireplace, elbows resting on his knees. In
front of him on the coffee table was a tray containing
cups, saucers, milk, sugar and a tea-cosy lying on its
side.

He was holding the panther, his expression absorbed
as he examined it.

As Shelley hesitated, the stair creaked and Adam
glanced up. Shelley felt an odd fluttering inside her.
He set the panther gently on the shelf above the
brightly burning fire and stood up.

Their eyes locked. Outside, the wind shrieked like a
soul in torment, rain lashed against the window and
the waves crashed and thundered against the quay.
Shelley swallowed audibly, feeling suddenly and
unaccountably nervous. He was looking at her in a
way she did not recognise, that made her feel warm
and tingly all over, that interfered with her breathing
and started a tremor in her hands.

He might own the cottage, thanks to Great-Uncle
Nicholas, but it was *her* home. It was small and low-
ceilinged, unlike anywhere Adam had lived. And yet,
standing beside the fireplace, he looked completely at
ease, as though he belonged.

Shelley felt trapped. But how, after all he had done
to help, getting himself soaked in the process, could
she possibly say, 'Thanks very much, but I want you
to leave now.' And was that honestly what she wanted?
The water was several inches deep on the quay and
still rising, for the tide would not reach its height for
another half an hour. In her heart of hearts, she did
not want to face that alone. Yet it might be several

hours before the water went down and the storm abated.

Adam held out his hand. 'Come and get warm,' he said.

CHAPTER EIGHT

'No,' she blurted. 'I—I must get rid of these first.' She lifted the bundle of sodden clothing. 'Thanks for setting the tray. I'll make the tea now. I expect you could do with something to eat. I'm absolutely starving.' She could hear herself babbling. She had gone beyond hunger, her stomach was knotted with tension, but preparing a meal would keep her busy and him at arm's length.

'Shelley?' he spoke softly, but something in his voice made the skin between her shoulder-blades prickle. She turned in the kitchen doorway.

'Yes?'

'Are you frightened of me?'

She hesitated only an instant, then laughed, a brittle sound. 'Don't be ridiculous!' She moistened suddenly dry lips. 'Omelette suit you?'

He shrugged. 'Fine,' he agreed, and started towards her. 'I'll give you a hand.'

'No,' she said desperately. 'I can manage, really.' He was too big and the kitchen too small. 'You—you'd better get out of those wet clothes.'

He raised one dark brow in mocking surprise. 'It did cross my mind,' he agreed, 'but I thought you might jump to the wrong conclusion if you came down and found me naked in front of the fire.' Shelley felt her cheeks flame. 'It seems I was mistaken.'

With a swift movement he tugged the sweater over his head and tossed it on to the back of the sofa. His skin gleamed copper-gold in the lamplight and the dancing flames formed an aura around him. Dark hair covered his broad chest, arrowing down across his flat stomach.

Shelley curled her nails into her palm, fighting an almost irresistible urge to reach out and touch him. Her eyes widened as his hands went to his belt and began to unbuckle it. He was taunting her, it was there in the quality of his smile. She wanted to outface him, but suddenly could not.

'No,' she said quickly, taking a swift step backward, 'that wasn't—I didn't——' Her face burned. 'I meant, why don't you go upstairs and have a shower? There's still plenty of hot water. While you're doing that, I'll get the meal ready.'

Perfectly relaxed, he let his arms fall to his sides, leaving the belt undone. His eyes were dark pools reflecting the flickering flame of the lamp.

Shelley's gaze slid away, too vulnerable to his probing stare. She focused on the panther and her throat constricted. They were one, man and beast, male animals in the peak of condition, alert, powerful and—each in his own way—deadly. She cleared her throat and turned towards the kitchen. 'You can dry your things by the fire.' It didn't sound like her voice. 'I'll fetch the clothes-horse. They won't take long.'

He shot her a sceptical look. 'Do you have a bathrobe I could borrow?' he enquired, so polite she knew he was laughing at her.

Reluctantly, she shook her head. 'You'd never get into mine.' Then, seeing the funny side of the situation, the corners of her mouth tilted upwards. 'Besides, I don't think satin-bound emerald velour is quite your style.'

'Maybe you're right,' he shrugged. 'You haven't anything else?' It sounded so casual. 'Nothing you keep for . . . ' the pause was infinitesimal, ' . . . guests?'

She shook her head again, not recognising the implication. 'No one's ever stayed here.'

'Hasn't it been lonely for you?' His tone was a perfect balance of polite enquiry and friendly concern.

Her first thought was to deny it, but that would be a lie, and why should she lie? 'Sometimes,' she admitted. 'But having people to stay wouldn't change that, even if I knew anyone well enough——' She broke off, looking down at the bundle in her hands, aware she had revealed more than she intended about the reality of her life since moving to Cornwall. 'Anyway,' she added quickly, 'loneliness is a mental state, not a physical one, and——' a note of defiance crept into her voice, '—I enjoy my own company.' She marched into the kitchen, dumped the bundle on the table and started back to the living-room, flinching as she almost collided with Adam, who filled the doorway. 'I—I'll fetch you a clean towel and a blanket you can wrap yourself in while your clothes dry.'

'I'll get them,' he offered, looking down at her. 'Just tell me——'

'No, I'll do it,' Shelley's voice was sharp. She didn't want him setting foot in her bedroom. It was the only retreat she had left. In that room she had begun the painful emotional process of rebuilding her life. How many nights had she cried into her pillow? But she had survived, had come to terms with herself and her new existence. Moreover, she had even begun to enjoy it.

There had been the odd black day when she had been possessed by a nameless yearning. But she had fought grimly, deliberately ignoring the fact that it usually assailed her after a tune, a smell, a scene, or a snatch of conversation had reminded her of him.

She had almost managed to convince herself that the only feeling she retained for Adam Trelawney was hatred. Almost. But if she allowed him to set foot in that room, there would be nowhere left to hide, nowhere untouched by the lingering imprint of his personality. He was here now. He had spoken of staying at least until the end of summer. But then what? The house would not necessarily hold him. He had bought and sold too many for one more to make a difference. Life down here would not suit him for long. He was used to pressure, challenge, making quick decisions involving huge sums of money. He would not stay.

Shelley hugged the folded blanket, resting her cheeks against its softness, inhaling the scent of sandalwood which permeated it from the storage box at the foot of her bed.

It would be easy, so dangerously easy, to get used to him being around. She had missed him terribly during those three days. Since that moment in his house when he had begun to make love to her, she had thought of him more than she dared remember, far more than was safe. They fought all the time, yet she had only to be with him to feel vibrantly, wholly alive.

She dropped the blanket and clean towel on top of the Ali Baba basket in the bathroom, and hurried downstairs.

Adam had just put more coal on the fire and stood up, turning to face her.

'All yours,' she said brightly, waving towards the stairs. As he moved towards her she edged quickly away and his mouth twisted. She watched as he crouched beside the front door, felt the towels, then pushed them tightly against the gap.

'Are they wet?' she forced herself to ask.

'Damp,' came the succinct reply. 'But there's only a few minutes to go and then the tide should start ebbing.' He put his foot on the bottom stair. 'Want to scrub my back?'

Shelley tossed her head and turned away before he could see the flush that warmed her cheeks.

'In that case I'll only be ten minutes. Oh, by the way,' his tone changed and she glanced over her shoulder. 'I saw your parents while I was in London. We spent a very pleasant evening together.' He continued up the stairs, leaving Shelley staring, open-mouthed, after him.

Wearing the blanket like a toga, Adam had refused to answer her questions while they ate. Shelley had been tempted to argue, to *demand* he tell her how the meeting had come about, and its outcome. But she realised almost at once the futility of such an approach.

Barely tasting the food, she felt her strength returning with each mouthful. Adam was talking about his house, outlining his plans for furniture and colour schemes. Half of Shelley's mind was totally caught up in what he was saying, seeing quite clearly the images his words conjured. The other half stood aside and watched him, the changing expressions on his hard-planed face, the way he used his hands—strong, capable hands—to define a shape or illustrate a point.

He pushed his empty plate away and turned to regard her with a slight frown. 'What do you think about a fitted carpet in the drawing-room?'

Shelley remembered the room, its beautiful proportions, the white marble fireplace and the long windows that looked over the estuary. She also remembered, with even greater clarity, the tartan rug on the bare floor, the remains of their picnic, and Adam's arms around her, his lips burning her throat, her breast . . . She thrust the thought away.

'Why ask me?' she said abruptly. 'It's your house.'

'Indeed,' came the calm reply. 'But you have an eye for blending——' he looked about him '—style and comfort.' His gaze returned to her. 'I was asking your *opinion,* not your advice. You won't be held responsible.'

His tone, and the implication, stung.

'I'm not afraid of responsibility,' Shelley responded tartly.

'Oh no?' His scepticism was plain.

'No!' Shelley snapped. 'I have—*had*——' she glanced at him '—a very successful business. I may not be in your income bracket, but I've no debts either.'

'Very commendable. But that wasn't what I meant.'

'Really. Then what do you mean?'

He didn't answer at once, and when he did his tone had softened. 'Don't you think this feud with your parents has gone on long enough?'

'That is none of your business.'

'They made it my business.'

'How?'

'They both said how much they miss you.'

Shelley gave a strangled laugh that was almost a sob.

'They also said they appreciated the fact you let them know you were safe and well.'

Shelley made an awkward gesture and began to collect up the dirty dishes. 'I didn't want them to worry.'

'No?' Again the scepticism.

'No!' she shouted. Then, with an effort, 'How are they?'

'Do you really care?'

Shelley flinched inwardly. 'Not much.' It wasn't true, she *did* care. She had hated the way she had left home, stealing away like a thief in the night. But there had been no alternative. They would not listen. They never had.

Adam's expression was bleak and contemptuous. 'I thought you said you had grown up.'

Shelley jerked round to face him, the dishes clattering as she knocked a cup over. 'So?'

'So listen to you, nursing your grudge, pampering it, keeping it well nourished with righteous indignation.'

Shelley jumped to her feet and, picking up the laden tray, marched out into the kitchen with it. She was seething. How dare he! She put the tray down, then stood still, her head bowed. It wasn't true. *It wasn't.*

When she returned to the living-room, Adam had moved the coffee table back against the wall and was rebuilding the fire. She could not get to her armchair so instead sank down on to the sofa, stiffening as he sat beside her. Half turning, he laid one arm along the sofa-back behind her head. She kept her head averted so he should not see her sudden nervousness.

'Rochelle, how will your parents ever know what you've achieved if you don't tell them, or better still, show them?'

She stole a sideways glance at him, her hands moving restlessly in her lap, her back rigid with tension.

'You told me you were doing what you wanted.' He sounded exasperated.

'I am,' she agreed.

'Then why not invite them down? Prove that you were right and they were wrong. You've got your career, and the independence you always wanted. You can afford to be generous.'

She glanced at him again. She hadn't looked at it like that. She had tried hard not to think about them at all, believing the gap unbridgable. But she had changed, hadn't she? Maybe they had, too. And even if they hadn't, she was secure enough in her own talent to be able to shrug off any criticism. 'I suppose I could,' she murmured uncertainly, then frowned. 'Why should you care? And how did you come to meet them?'

Adam leaned over, picked up his torch and handed it to Shelley.

'What's that for?' she asked, astonished.

'To shine in my eyes. That's how interrogations are usually conducted, I believe.'

Shelley bit her lip. 'Sorry.' She held the torch out to him and he placed it on the floor.

'Life's too short for vendettas, Rochelle. This

business has taken its toll of them both, but especially your father.'

Shelley felt a pang. 'There's nothing wrong, is there? He's not ill?'

Adam shook his head. 'To the best of my knowledge they're both fine. But your father looks older, a lot older. I think what hit him hardest was the fact that you sent your letters via a solicitor in London, so that they couldn't trace your whereabouts. This was one occasion when neither his money nor his network of connections were of any use. You had made a new life for yourself over which he had no control, and about which he knew nothing. That took some coming to terms with.'

His hand slid from the back of the sofa to rest lightly on her shoulder. 'I haven't told them where you are, Rochelle. I haven't even mentioned your name. Your father and I still have business arrangements, and it was in connection with those that we met and he invited me to dinner at Eaton Square. *He* brought the subject up.'

'Thank you,' she murmured, 'for not——'

'Thanks are not necessary,' he cut in brusquely. 'If you decide to get in touch with them, the decision must be wholly yours. I don't want your father thinking I pressured you into it.'

'Isn't that exactly what you *are* doing?' Shelley shot back.

His sudden grin was utterly disarming and Shelley's breath caught in her throat. 'Of course. But for *your* sake as much as theirs.' His smile faded. 'My parents are dead. It's too late for me to apologise for all the misunderstandings, to tell them they were right after all about so many things, and to prove to them that, despite their concern and doubts, I really did know what I was doing.'

He withdrew his arm and getting up, lifted the panther from the mantelpiece. As he sat down again, he was somehow closer. She could feel through the blanket the hard-muscled length of his thigh against hers. He turned the panther in his strong, sensitive fingers. It gleamed in the light of the dancing flames. 'You have a remarkable talent, Rochelle.' He did not look at her as he spoke, his gaze fixed on the sleek cat.

Shelley felt something akin to joy flower within her. It wasn't just the words, but the tone in which they were spoken. She had never expected admiration from Adam, and it echoed like sweet music in her ears. He turned his head, his eyes meeting hers.

'I never realised.'

In that quiet sentence she recognised apology and explanation.

'I know,' she replied simply. 'I wasn't as good—then. I've had a lot of practice, and made a lot of mistakes, in the last three years.'

He lifted the panther. 'Have you made many of these?'

She shook her head, silently.

He stared at it, his brows contracting. 'Strange,' he murmured as if to himself, 'I get the oddest feeling——' He flicked a glance at her. 'How many?'

Her throat was uncomfortably dry, but she shrugged with apparent carelessness. 'Only that one.'

'Do you plan to make any more?'

'No.' It came as a whisper. Even if she tried, she knew she could never repeat it. Like Adam, the panther was unique.

'Rochelle, will you sell it to me?' he asked quietly.

She swallowed. 'Why do you want it?'

He looked at the sleek, black shape, smoothed it. 'I could say I want it because you wouldn't sell me the heron, or because one day soon your work will become famous and this piece will be very valuable, or even because it would look magnificent on the white marble of my drawing-room mantelpiece. All of those are valid reasons.' He looked up, his eyes very dark.

'But?' she murmured, the question drawn from her against her will. She was moving on to highly dangerous ground, yet, like a siren song, it beckoned her onward and she had not the strength or the will to resist.

'But they aren't the reasons I want it.'

'Then—why?' Shelley's expression must have reflected something of her turmoil, for Adam lifted one hand and drew his index finger lightly down her face from temple to chin. The brief movement, totally unexpected, was oddly tender.

He set the panther on the wooden shelf above the fireplace, and Shelley found herself staring at it. In the glow of the leaping flames it looked almost alive. Its lowered head, flattened ears and snarling muzzle, though miniature, still exuded enough power, enough threat, to send an icy shiver down her spine.

Adam sat back and lifted Shelley's trembling hands in his own. The blanket had slipped from his shoulder. She could feel the warmth of his skin, smell the soap he had used. Her soap.

'Look at me.' She obeyed. 'I want that sculpture because it has a piece of your soul in it.'

Shelley's heart kicked painfully and she caught her breath.

'Your other work is good,' he said, 'very good. But the panther is special. Name your price, Rochelle. I'll pay you whatever you ask.'

She stared at him, shaken and speechless. Thoughts flew through her mind at the speed of light. He would keep his word, that she knew. He was also extremely wealthy. He wouldn't miss a few hundred, or even thousand pounds, and that sort of money would solve so many of her problems—a place to work for one. Adam could build his block of flats, while she established a new gallery somewhere nearer the centre of town. It would be a perfectly legal transaction with

no strings attached. She would be totally independent
at last. Her worries would be over.

Shelley lowered her head, knowing even as the
thoughts occurred, that she could not accept his offer.
The independence she valued so highly had little to
do with money. It concerned peace of mind and a
knowledge of what was right. Her mouth widened
fractionally in a wry, tired smile. She shook her head.
'It's not for sale.'

He caught her chin and jerked her head up, his face
hard. 'Don't tell me you don't need money. I know
you've survived on a shoe-string.'

'Oh? How do you know?' She pulled her chin free.

'Never mind,' he snapped. 'Well?'

'I never said I didn't need money,' Shelley replied.
'I said the panther is not for sale.' She swallowed.
'But you may have it—as a gift.'

Adam looked startled, then suspicion narrowed his
eyes, but so briefly that Shelley wasn't really certain
she had seen it at all. 'You're *giving* it to me? *Why?*'

What could she say? Because you inspired it?
Because if I keep it, it will be a constant reminder of
you, and that is something I cannot afford?

She moistened her lips and shrugged, suddenly very
weary. 'A token of thanks for your help this evening.
Despite what I said earlier, I—I couldn't have coped
on my own, what with Elsie and Frank and everything.' Resting her head against the back of the sofa,
she stifled a yawn. 'What a day!'

'Are you sure—about the panther?'

She smiled at the doubt in his voice. It may not
have been a wise move from a business point of view,
but she had taken the wind right out of Adam Trelawney's sails, and that alone made it worthwhile. Besides,
she had meant what she said. She nodded, staring into
the flames. She was warm and comfortable, and for
once she and Adam weren't fighting. The storm seemed
far, far away. She sighed.

'Then let me thank *you*,' he said softly and, as she rolled her head sideways to tell him it wasn't necessary, he kissed her.

Her hands flew up to fend him off, but, touching his bare skin, she jerked back as if scalded. For one fatal instant she hesitated and after that it was too late.

As his lips brushed hers again and again, sending tiny shocks out to her toes and fingertips, she rested her hands on his shoulders, exploring the texture of his skin, feeling the play of taut muscles beneath its surface.

His mouth grew more demanding. She felt herself moving as he eased her sideways and his body half covered hers as she lay flat against the cushions. Of their own volition her arms slid round him, welcoming him as he held her close. She smoothed the thick, springing hair curling on his neck, still damp from the shower, and floated on a swelling sea of sensuality. His tongue parted her lips and gently probed her mouth, and a shaft of exquisite sweetness pierced her.

With a wordless moan she clung to him. Her senses reeled and she could scarcely breathe. The storm was no longer outside. It was in the room, inside *her*. She knew now that this was what she had yearned for, *this man*. The hostility, the apprehension and feeling of threat had been but a smoke-screen, her mind's attempt to disguise the truth. She still loved him.

He relinquished her mouth and pressed burning lips to her temple, her eyes and her throat. Loosening the ribbon that held back her hair, he grasped a handful and tugged, pulling her head back as, with a hoarse mutter, his teeth grazed her chin and he claimed her mouth once more.

She sensed his growing excitement and found herself responding helplessly. His heart thudded against her breast and beneath her palms his skin was hot and slippery.

She gasped, the sound catching as a whimper in her throat, as Adam reached beneath her shirt. His fingers were deliciously cool on her fevered skin as he caressed her with a lightness and delicacy that made her quiver and arch against him.

He tore his mouth from hers, his breathing laboured. 'Rochelle,' he muttered hoarsely, 'I want you so much, I——' He was interrupted by a loud banging on the wall.

For a moment neither moved or breathed. Shelley didn't understand what had happened. Seconds later there was another thunderous tattoo. Then it came to her. 'Oh, my God!' she croaked, 'I forgot—Elsie.'

'What about her?' Adam demanded, his eyes glittering, his face dark and hungry.

Shelley licked her swollen lips. 'She asked me to knock on the wall to let her know I was all right. I forgot all about it.'

Muttering an expletive that sent Shelley's cheeks pink even as she echoed its sentiment, Adam raised himself and swung round. With bowed head, he rested his elbows on his knees and pushed shaking hands through his hair. 'Dear Elsie,' he grated. 'Dear, caring, thoughtful Elsie. *I could strangle her.*'

Shelley started to giggle. She knew she shouldn't, but she couldn't stop, the tension was too great to contain. If she didn't laugh, she would cry, or scream, or throw things.

Adam stood up, glaring fiercely at her. She stood up more slowly, slightly light-headed. She ached inside and knew he must feel even worse. She laid one hand on his chest in a gesture that said all she could not put into words.

Suddenly he relaxed. His stony expression cracked into a wry grin as he raised both fists and shook them at the low ceiling. Then, proving his reflexes were as sharp as ever, he caught the blanket before it fell about his ankles.

Turning away, her face warm, her pulses still pounding, Shelley picked up the brass poker and, reaching into the alcove, banged three times with the handle.

She had just replaced the poker on the hearth when the knocking came again, this time through the kitchen wall. She looked up at Adam, frowning in concern.

He glanced at his watch. 'The tide has been ebbing almost an hour. If she was flooded, she'd have let you know before now.'

Shelley blinked at him. *How could she have forgotten?* The storm, the spring tide, her cold exhaustion and the misery of the past week had all paled into insignificance once Adam had arrived.

'It might be an idea to check the towels,' he pointed towards the front door and Shelley darted round the sofa as he went into the kitchen.

'Mrs Penfold!' he shouted, hammering on the wall, 'Open your back door!'

'They're both saturated,' Shelley panted as she wrung them out, one at a time, as hard as she could into the sink.

'Seepage from the sandbags, or sea water getting through?' he queried.

'I didn't wait to see,' Shelley replied and dashed back to jam the towels in place. Some water had oozed under the door in the few seconds she had been away, but as she mopped it up and wadded the towels firmly against the gap, Shelley refused to worry. The tide was on its way out and the wind would have changed before the next high.

She heard Adam shout to Elsie once more, and ran back into the kitchen just as he pulled the blanket more firmly round his shoulders before opening the back door.

'Mrs Penfold, can you hear me?' he bellowed.

'Mr Trelawney? Is that you?' Elsie's voice sounded thin against the gusting wind. 'I see the rain's easing

off a bit. Not so bad as it was backlong. I never 'eard
you come.'

Shelley hid a smile at Elsie's tone which registered
both annoyance at having missed the event, and a
burning curiosity. 'All right, are 'ee?'

'We're fine,' Adam shouted. 'Is everything OK with
you? Do you need anything?'

'No, I'm all right. Worried 'bout Shelley, I was. But
she'll be fine now you're there. You 'ad the water in?'

'No.' Adam glanced round at Shelley. 'Any
messages?' he grinned. She shook her head. 'Sorry,
what was that?' he yelled out of the door.

'I said, are you going to be there all night, just in
case anything do go wrong?'

'Yes,' he shouted, and Shelley felt an odd contrac-
tion within her. 'Don't worry, Mrs Penfold, the worst
is over. I'll see you in the morning. Goodnight.'

''Night, my 'andsome.'

Hearing Elsie's door slam, Adam quietly closed the
cottage door and slid home the bolt. Then he turned
towards Shelley who had begun unloading the tray,
her head bent. Suddenly she felt very uncertain.

'It will be all over the town tomorrow,' she warned,
not looking at him.

'Sorry?' His thoughts were obviously elsewhere.
'What will?'

'That you spent the night here.' She shot him a
brief glance.

There was a moment's silence, then he said, 'Which
bothers you most, Rochelle, my staying, or it becoming
public knowledge?'

She shrugged hesitantly. 'I—it's—well, you might
have asked me first,' she blurted and turned back to
the washing up.

In a couple of strides Adam was behind her, his
hands on her shoulders, thumbs gently massaging the
back of her neck. Immediately, some of the tension
left her. 'You're absolutely right. I'm sorry, I just

didn't think. Would you rather I left? I can always sleep in the car.'

She looked round quickly. 'Why the car?'

He pulled a wry face. 'I can't get back to the hotel, the road's still blocked by fallen trees. One just missed me on my way here.'

Shelley's eyes widened. 'Oh, I'd no idea——'

'Of course you didn't.' He was mildly impatient. 'I didn't tell you, and you already had your hands full. Listen,' his voice softened, 'there's nothing to worry about. We're both very tired. I'll be on the sofa, you'll be upstairs.'

'It's just that——'

'I know,' he cut in, stroking her hair back from her face. 'As for Elsie gossiping, what does it matter? *We* know the truth.'

'Your reputation will be compromised,' she warned, only half joking.

He made a brief, dismissive movement. 'So will yours,' he replied. 'Does that concern you?'

She laughed shortly. 'Aren't artists supposed to do this sort of thing all the time?' She turned back to the sink. 'I guess I'm just a late starter.'

He spun her round so fast that hot water and bubbles sprayed over the kitchen floor. 'There'll be no others, Rochelle. Only me.'

Later, lying in bed, unable to sleep despite her exhaustion, Shelley stared at the ceiling. The rain had stopped, and the wind, though still strong, no longer blew directly on to the cottage. She could hear the waves crashing against the quay wall and spray hissed and splattered over the top. Even after the storm had passed, the sea would remain rough for a day or two, but she was used to that.

Was Adam asleep? she wondered. He deserved to be. What a day it must have been for him. First the drive back from London, then almost being hit by a falling tree on his way over, and, to cap it all, getting soaked to the skin by gale-driven, freezing rain, sandbagging the door of people he hadn't even met.

She had found him a toothbrush, the one she had bought to take away on holiday and forgotten, and had laughed at his patent relief when she explained that though the sofa did not convert into a proper bed, the arms folded down flat to allow him to stretch out.

When they said goodnight she had hesitated, wondering if he would kiss her. Wanting him to, yet wary. But after looking at her intently for a moment, he had merely turned her round and given her a gentle push towards the stairs. 'Go to bed, Rochelle,' he had growled, 'before I forget my good intentions. We both need some sleep.'

Shelley turned over and snuggled into the pillow. He was right. There would be plenty of time to talk, to love, to re-learn all that had been forgotten, and discover what had never been known, in the weeks ahead. Everything was different now. There was no longer any point in denying that she loved him. The way he had kissed her, the things he had said must mean he felt the same way. The barriers were crumbling. Soon they would be swept completely away. Soon, for the first time, he would tell her what was in his heart.

Smiling, Shelley closed her eyes and, with a happy sigh, fell asleep.

When she woke the following morning she felt marvellous, and for a moment could not imagine why. Then it all flooded back. Bounding out of bed she opened the window and bright sunlight filled the room. The aftermath of the storm was evident in the low, fast-moving clouds and heaving waves. But, as forecast, the wind had gone round to the west and there was plenty of blue sky.

Washed and dressed, her hair held back in two combs, her face bare of make-up, Shelley went downstairs.

Adam was still fast asleep, lying on his back, the blanket pushed down to his waist and his feet sticking out of the end. One arm was bent over his head, the other flung out sideways. With tousled hair and the harsh planes of his face softened in total relaxation, he looked oddly vulnerable. Shelley's heart skipped a beat as she looked down at him. She had never seen him like this. It was a moment to treasure.

As if sensing her presence, he stirred. Too shy to be caught staring, she went to the window and drew back the curtains. Adam groaned and muttered. Then, as Shelley turned to face him, with snake-like speed, his arm shot out, grabbed her hand and jerked her towards him. In the same instant he sat up. His arms enfolded her and his mouth fastened on hers. He was warm from sleep and his kiss was sweet-tasting and tender.

Crushed against his bare chest, she felt the steady thud of his heartbeat and the rising heat in his body. When he released her they were both breathless.

'I thought I'd dreamed it all,' he murmured and, lifting her hand, pressed his lips to her palm. Trembling inside, Shelley caressed his ruffled curls. With an effort she drew her hands away.

'Breakfast?' Her voice was husky.

He looked up at her, his eyes gleaming. 'You cook as well?' He ducked the blow she aimed at him and made a lunge for her. Laughing, blissfully happy, she jumped back out of reach.

'Orange juice, muesli, toast, bacon and eggs, tea or coffee?'

'Yes, please.'

'You're supposed to choose.'

'I just did. All of it, and coffee.'

Shelley shrugged and, folding her arms, grinned at him. 'Not much wrong with your appetite.'

'No,' he agreed, his hands linked about his blanket-covered knees. 'In fact, I'm getting hungrier by the minute.' The feral glitter in his narrowed eyes as they swept over her left no doubt as to the true meaning of his words and Shelley was assailed by a delicious weakness.

'Your clothes should be dry by now,' she said over her shoulder as she went into the kitchen to fill the kettle. There was a faint tremor in her hands as she began to prepare breakfast for them both.

'Do I get the impression you're trying to tell me something?' Swathed in the blanket, Adam filled the doorway. His hand rasped over the black stubble on his chin.

'Only that Elsie will probably be round any minute to make sure we're both OK,' Shelley retorted drily.

Adam's smile was ironic. 'But surely this is what she'll be *expecting* to see?'

'Quite possibly. But,' Shelley gestured helplessly, 'we don't *have* to advertise——'

'It's all right,' he broke in gently. 'I was only teasing. I'll go and dress right away.'

She flashed him a grateful smile that faltered at the sound of a knock on the front door.

He shrugged. 'Too late, I'm afraid.'

Shelley started forward. 'I'll go——' But he caught her arm.

'We've nothing to hide, Rochelle. Anyway, why spoil her fun? You get on with breakfast. *I'll* go.' Before she could argue, he had disappeared.

As she opened the fridge to get the bacon, she heard the door open and listened for Elsie's reaction.

'Oh!' She froze. It was Gary's voice. 'I—I just came to see if Shell was all right.'

'She's fine.' Adam's voice was icily polite.

'I was worried—the storm and everything.' Shelley clutched the bacon. How *young* he sounded.

'A little late, don't you think?'

'I—I want to speak to her,' Gary said desperately.

'I'm afraid she's busy right now,' Adam replied.

'Cooking my breakfast.'

Shelley closed her eyes. Poor Gary!

'Well,' she heard him mumble, 'tell her I called.'

'Of course.' Adam closed the door.

CHAPTER NINE

WHEN Shelley arrived at the Gallery an hour later than usual and breathless, Kath and Gary were already there. Both were packing.

Before he had left, Adam had dismantled the barrier from all three doorways, leaving the sandbags in front of the wall to drain. He had made her promise not to try moving them, saying he would see to it later. Then, with black stubble covering the lower half of his face, looking more like a tramp than a millionaire property developer in his stained and creased clothes, he had departed for the hotel. But first he had given her a long, lingering kiss that made her toes curl and her heart race.

She was glowing with happiness as she pushed open the glass door. But her smile faded as Gary looked up, his expression bitter and full of resentment.

Shelley met his gaze, her head high, sorry for the hurt he was so obviously suffering, but not prepared to assume a guilt she had no reason to feel.

He glared at her and opened his mouth. But thinking better of whatever he had been going to say, his jaw snapped shut and he bent his head, giving his attention to the bags, wallets and key-rings he was packing into a cardboard box.

Kath's gaze darted from one to the other. She raised her eyebrows in silent question at Shelley, who lifted one shoulder in a gesture of helplessness.

Dropping her bag on to her stool, Shelley went over to Kath who was folding richly patterned sweaters and jackets into tissue paper before placing them in a large suitcase. 'Everything OK?'

Kath beamed at her. 'Fantastic. Auntie's taken a whole new lease of life. She's got the decorators in and has threatened the poor painter with all sorts of terrible things if my workroom isn't finished by the time I get back.'

'I know your work- and saleroom is at the front of the house, but how does she feel about people walking in and out all day? From what you told me I always imagined she was a very private person.'

Kath laughed. 'She was. But now she's all prepared to offer potential customers a cup of tea. She says it makes the business more personal and friendly, and, the customers will feel honour-bound to buy something!'

'I think your auntie could teach some city tycoons a thing or two,' Shelley grinned.

'Yes, well, I've managed to put her off by pointing out that *she* would have to do all the tea-making and washing up as I would be far too busy spinning, knitting and discussing commissions. Still, if I can keep a firm hand on my business, Auntie will be a real help, and I'll have no more worries about her being alone. I hadn't realised how low she was.' Kath held a folded sweater to her chest. 'I was so caught up in my own problems, I hadn't noticed how withdrawn she had become. The difference now is amazing. At this rate she'll see *me* off!'

'I'm so glad it's all worked out for you, Kath.' Shelley meant every word.

'What about you? Have you found anywhere else yet?'

Shelley shook her head. 'But something will turn up. I'm sure it will.'

Kath looked thoughtfully round the Gallery. 'We had a lot of good times here, Shelley. It was hard work, but it was a lot of fun, too. I wish it hadn't had to end this way, but at least some good has come out of it. John would never have moved to Newlyn off his own bat, yet he and Sue will probably do much better down there. Auntie's on cloud nine. She's great company—she's got this wicked sense of humour.'

Shelley smiled. 'You're a very kind person, Kath. I hope she appreciates you.'

Kath lowered her voice and bent close. 'I thought perhaps you and Gary——' She let the words trail off, half-statement, half-question.

Sadly, Shelley shook her head again. 'It wouldn't have worked. I guess all this brought it to a head.'

'What about Adam Trelawney?' Kath's gaze was shrewd. 'What does he want? And I'm not referring to the Gallery.'

Shelley's cheeks grew warm. 'I'm not sure—yet. But something good has come out of this for me, too. I—I'm going to write to my parents and invite them down.'

Kath gripped her hand. 'Oh, Shelley, I'm *so* glad.'

Shelley grimaced. 'I don't know if they'll come. Perhaps this isn't the right time to ask them. After all, the Gallery's being demolished and I've nowhere else to go, yet.'

Kath shook her gently. 'What does that matter? The important thing is that you're contacting them. What they do is up to them. But *you've* made the first move and that's the worst hurdle over. Good luck, Shelley. I hope it turns out all right.'

Shelley smiled nervously. 'So do I,' she murmured, 'so do I,' and returned to her work area.

As she stood, undecided, staring at her crowded bench, Gary fitted the wooden lid on his machine with a loud clatter and locked it. Stuffing the key into his pocket, he strode towards the door.

Moved by the sight of his strained expression, Shelley turned. 'Gary——' she began, but he pushed straight past her.

'Bitch,' he muttered, and Shelley winced as though

he had struck her. Her face flamed and tears pricked her eyelids.

'I thought you wanted to speak to me.' She did not raise her voice and felt both pride and relief that it remained level, revealing none of the turmoil she was experiencing.

He stopped. 'That was this morning. But you were too busy,' he almost choked. 'I suppose *he'd* been there all night?' The words were wrung from him.

'Yes.' Shelley looked him straight in the eye. 'The road was blocked and he was soaked through. He'd sandbagged my door and one of my neighbours'. I couldn't have managed without his help. No one else came.'

'I didn't know——' Gary began defensively, but Shelley cut him off.

'That wasn't a criticism, it was a simple statement of fact. So is this. Adam spent the night on my sofa. Now you can believe that or not, I don't care. But if you're angry enough to be so rude to me, at least be honest about the reason.' She turned back to her bench and, with hands that trembled slightly, began to collect the longer shards of glass, placing them in a wide-mouthed jar. After a moment's silence, she heard his swift footsteps receding, then the door slammed.

She drew in a shaky sigh. Remaining here any longer was pointless. She hadn't had a customer for days and the contractors were due within a week.

At four o'clock, Gary reappeared in a battered blue van, driven by a young man with a punk haircut, wearing patched jeans and an over-large donkey-jacket. He parked right outside her window and when she looked out he leered and winked at her. Between them, he and Gary carried out hides, tools, the machine, and the boxes containing the finished goods, and loaded them into the van. Then, giving her a cheeky wave, the friend climbed into the driver's seat and flicked on a transistor radio resting on the shelf above the dashboard. Shelley heard the blast of pop music and wondered how his hearing withstood the assault.

Lifting her models one by one off the display shelves in the window, she wrapped them in tissue paper before placing them carefully in a box containing wood shavings lying on her bench. She heard the door open and glanced up as Gary came back in, then carried on with what she was doing.

'Er—the—er——' he cleared his throat, '—the key.'

She looked up again. 'Thank you.' He dropped it into her hand.

His mouth worked. 'I'm sorry, Shell,' he muttered, shamefaced. 'Guess I'm a lousy loser.'

She gave him a small, sympathetic smile. 'Good luck, Gary. I'll miss you.'

He stuck both hands in his pockets. 'Yeah. Listen, Shell,' he seemed to be having difficulty finding the right words, 'this last couple of days—well——'

'It's OK,' she said. 'Let's just forget them.'

He grinned with relief. 'I was hoping you'd say that. Those three years were good, I've got a lot of happy memories.'

'Me, too.' She smiled at him.

The driver gave three long blasts on the horn and, as they looked out, beckoned impatiently.

'I'd better go.' Leaning forward, Gary planted an uncertain kiss just below Shelley's right eye. 'Friends?'

She nodded, touched. 'Friends.'

He paused at the door. 'If you ever need me, Shell, no strings, I promise—well, you know where I am.'

She watched him drive off in a cloud of exhaust and heavy metal. She was glad he had come round. They had been through a lot together. She would always care what happened to him, be interested in what he was doing and how he was getting on, but *need* him? She thought of Adam and her lips curved as her heart swelled with love and happiness. He was the only man she would ever need.

A few minutes later he walked in. She looked up, face aglow. 'I was just thinking about you.'

'Unmentionable things, I hope.' His eyes gleamed and delight shivered through her. 'Look, can you leave that for now?'

'Yes, I suppose so. Why?'

'There's something I want you to see.' He glanced at his watch. 'Only we'll have to hurry or it will mean waiting until tomorrow.'

He held her arm protectively as they hurried down the hill and out along the main street. Shelley stole a glance at him and thought yet again how handsome he was. His jaw was shaved smooth, and his black hair almost tamed by a comb. He was wearing chocolate-brown trousers and a fawn polo-neck beneath his sheepskin. Each time he leaned towards her to point out storm damage, she caught the elusive fragrance of his aftershave and breathed in deeply, wanting to absorb him into every part of her being.

They stopped at the entrance to a shopping arcade. 'What do you think of it?' he asked, indicating the first shop on the left-hand side of the entrance. The paintwork was flaking and the window that looked out on to the street had plainly not been cleaned for some time. Several rolls of material were displayed on a rack inside the window and had been there so long the sun had bleached most of the colour from them.

'Well, I've never actually bought anything in there,' Shelley replied carefully, not sure what he was driving at.

'I'm not surprised. I doubt if Mr Bowen has acquired any new stock in the last five years. But I was referring to the shop itself, the location.'

'Oh, that.' Shelley sighed. 'Now if only *I* could find somewhere like that——'

'Why *like* that? Why not *that* shop?'

'Because,' she explained with a touch of impatience,

'that shop belongs to Charles Bowen. It's been in his
family for generations. He took it over from his
grandfather after his father died of a heart attack in
the Plume of Feathers. Dozens of people have tried to
buy it and he's always refused to sell.'

'Not this time.'

It took several seconds for Shelley to realise what
Adam had said. Her head flew round. 'You mean——?'
She couldn't continue.

He nodded blandly. 'I mean.'

Shelley's gaze flew back once more to the shop. It
would be *perfect*. It was right in the centre of the
town. The window fronting the street was large enough
not only for a display, but also for her to be seen
working. Also, there was another window alongside
the door in which she could arrange a lighted exhibition.

She could feel him watching her, and waiting.

'Have you any plans for the shop, Adam?' she
enquired with a coolness that barely covered her
surging excitement.

He shrugged. 'I've tossed a few ideas around.
Nothing definite. Do you have any suggestions?'

'How about re-selling it, to me?' She held her
breath, fully expecting him, after making some crack,
to agree. Disappointment was sharp when he shook
his head. 'Oh!' She bit her lip, then smiled ruefully.
Adam was a businessman. He would not buy a
property to sell it again at once. No doubt Charles
Bowen had demanded a high price. Without spending
even more on repairs and redecoration Adam would
be unlikely to make a profit. Besides, it was open to
question whether she could afford it. 'How about a
lease, then?' That made far more sense.

He appeared to consider for a moment, pursing his
lips, then shook his head again.

Baffled and oddly hurt, Shelley strove to keep her
voice expressionless. If this was a game, it was rather

cruel. 'Well, it's obviously none of my business——'

'On the contrary,' his voice was rich with laughter, 'it's *entirely* your business, though I don't suppose you'll find much use for the stock.'

Shelley stared at him, perplexed. 'Adam, I don't understand. What are you saying?'

Gripping her shoulders, he turned her round to face the little shop. His breath was warm on her cheek, his voice deep and soft in her ear. 'The shop is yours, Rochelle. My gift to you.'

Like a brilliant firework, her delight soared skyward, then slowly died and fell back to earth, dark and spent. She swivelled round, her eyes wide. 'I can't,' she whispered.

'It's settled.'

For one instant, temptation tugged at her. She pulled free and turned to face him. 'Then you'll just have to unsettle it. Adam, I—I appreciate the gesture, really I do. But I can't accept, I'm sorry.'

During the pause that followed he regarded her steadily. 'I'm not your father, Rochelle.'

She could almost have laughed. Indeed he was not. 'Same tactics,' she whispered.

'And you won't compromise that independence of yours?'

She shrugged helplessly. 'I can't. Not where my work is concerned.'

'You mean,' he grinned, 'everything else is open to negotiation?'

She rubbed her forehead. It was beginning to ache. 'You're not angry?'

He shook his head and sighed in resignation. 'It was more or less what I expected. So, now you've seen the shop, let's say hello to Mr Bowen, who is moving out this evening. Then we'll go back to your cottage and hammer out a tenancy agreement that will satisfy you and to which I will reluctantly agree. After that, I'll take you to dinner.'

Oblivious to the amused passers-by, Shelley flung her arms round him. He really *did* understand.

That moment marked the beginning of the greatest happiness Shelley had ever known.

Money had always equalled power, and Adam could get things done immediately for which other people had to wait days or even weeks. Within three days the little shop had been painted inside and out. Among the bolts of cloth, Shelley had found an undamaged length of midnight-blue velvet which she used to dress the front window, taking it smoothly around the deep sides, and arranging it in soft folds across the bottom. It made a perfect frame for the spotlit display stands, and emphasised the delicacy of the sculptures which were attracting great interest.

The small back room provided an excellent store. She was even able to keep the gas and air bottles in there out of the way, piping the mixture to the lamp on her bench.

She had spent the whole of one evening trying to compose a letter to her parents, scrapping draft after draft, almost giving up as her confidence was suffocated by the doubts that reared up to taunt her. Adam had arrived close on ten o'clock and, seeing her miserable and surrounded by crumpled paper, had clasped her to him, laughing.

'You idiot!' His expression was tender as he tilted her chin with his index finger. 'Hasn't it occurred to you that *they'll* be nervous? They might not show it. They're both used to hiding behind a "social" face. But inside——' He shook his head. 'They'll be on *your* territory here and at the shop. There's nothing to worry about, Rochelle. You'll have them eating out of your hand.'

Within ten minutes, Shelley had penned a brief but warm note and sealed it ready for posting the following day. As they sprawled comfortably on the sofa, their feet stretched out towards the fire, Adam had brought her up to date regarding the work on his house. Later, when their kisses had fanned the smouldering embers of their mutual need into fierce flames, he had abruptly broken free of her embrace. With trembling hands and a smile that did not reach his eyes, he had gone, leaving her bewildered and aching for him.

Several days later, Elsie invited them both in to inspect her wall, newly repaired by the builder Adam had engaged. Delighted with the work, Elsie's pleasure had been greatly enhanced by the builder confiding in her his troubles, which were considerable, since his wife had left him to set up home with a long-distance lorry driver who, *everyone* knew, had other 'wives' wherever his stop-over was longer than two days.

As Elsie mused aloud on the source of such stamina, Adam caught Shelley's eye and she had to pretend a sudden bout of coughing to smother her giggles. Once the subject of the builder was exhausted, Elsie had turned her sharp gaze on Adam and, to Shelley's shocked embarrassment, had begun singing *her* praises as a prospective wife for him.

It was one thing to harbour such dreams and hopes herself, but something else entirely to hear Elsie cataloguing her virtues as though she were a mare at a bloodstock sale.

Adam was no help. Clearly enjoying himself, he was actively encouraging Elsie, but when she mentioned 'good child-bearing hips' Shelley had had enough. With scarlet cheeks, and the rest of her uncomfortably warm, she had dragged Adam out into the sunshine, mortification battling with her sense of humour. Adam's protestations of innocence were so blatantly outrageous that laughter won, and when he kissed her outside her front door and whispered that Elsie had told him nothing he had not already learned for himself, her joy reached new heights.

But he still did not make love to her.

They went to his house and she was stunned by the

transformation. 'You must have had an army working here to get all this done so quickly,' she gasped as he led her from room to room.

From the oak panelling and leather chairs of the study, they crossed the spacious hall. Peach walls, gleaming white paintwork and a pine-green carpet that extended up the curving staircase, made it warm and welcoming. The dining-room was formal with rich mahogany and pale gold brocade.

Opening the double doors, Adam stood back, motioning Shelley to precede him into the drawing-room. The wood floor gleamed with a patina of wax polish and was only partly covered by the Oriental carpet of pink, cream and brown. The covers on the comfortable-looking sofa and armchairs picked up the same colours, with an added touch of turquoise, echoed in the floor-length velvet curtains held back by silk ropes. Pearl-grey walls, an ornate low table of gilt and glass, and a black lacquered cabinet added their own elegance. It was exactly as he had said it would be. She could not have improved on it. Undoubtedly luxurious, it was none the less a home rather than a house, a place in which to be comfortable and at peace.

'No comment?' Adam enquired and Shelley spread her hands.

'What can I say? It's beautiful, Adam, the colours, the furniture, everything.' Her sweeping glance lighted on the fireplace. There, in pride of place on the cool white marble mantelpiece, crouched the panther.

'Magnificent, isn't he?' Adam said quietly. 'He looks well in here.'

Shelley nodded. It was the ideal setting for them both. Envy knifed through her. The longing to be part of it, to live in this house with Adam, was a physical pain. It had nothing to do with the size or luxury of the place. Her parents' flat in Eaton Square had possessed more than enough of both. She did not understand her own reaction. Her cottage had meant everything to her. It had been her retreat, her security, her independence.

She smiled up at him, thrusting the thought to the back of her mind. 'Can I look upstairs?'

'No. It's . . . not quite finished yet,' he explained and, clasping her hand, led her outside to see how the garden reclamation was progressing.

By the time he took her home that evening, Shelley was deeply impressed, not only by what he had achieved in such an incredibly short time, but by his vision and taste. There was no ostentatious display of wealth, yet everything was of the best, a quiet but definite statement of quality.

But gradually, insidiously, moments of dejection began to infiltrate her new-found happiness. She felt a growing uncertainty.

Adam was making a point of seeing her every day, even if it was only for a nightcap. He wanted to know about her new designs, who had come into the shop and what they had bought. He brushed aside her apprehension at not having received a reply from her parents. His explanation—that leading busy and mainly separate lives, it took time to alter their appointments and arrange several days when both were free—was both logical and comforting.

Sharing the details of his day with her, he talked not only about progress on the house, but about projects his company was involved in. The demolition team had razed the Gallery and structural engineers were overseeing the installation of foundations for the block of flats. But when he offered to take her up to see, Shelley declined. The memories were still too fresh. Adam seemed to understand and shrugged it off with a smile. He had not wanted her to feel excluded.

In fact, that was the very heart of the problem. He had become, once more, an integral part of her life. When they kissed, the effect upon them both was

profound. He was not faking his reaction, she would
stake her life on that. She loved him with every fibre
of her being and made no effort to hide her feelings.
Though, because of his own reticence on the subject,
she held back the words she so longed to say, not
wanting to presume or pressure him in any way. But
when he held her and his mouth was a sweet torment,
her heart cried out to him, *I love you, Adam.*

He had invited her into every area of his life,
discussing his home and his work in greater detail
than ever before. Yet more and more as the days
passed, she felt she was only an observer. Never by
word or deed, did he make her feel that she was *part*
of it.

Thus, the shadows deepened in Shelley's eyes and
some of the joy went out of her smile. In so many
ways she and Adam were closer than they had ever
been. But in the one thing that really mattered, the
honest, fearless expression of their feelings for one
another, the invisible barrier remained unbreached
and he was still a stranger.

One Saturday morning a few weeks later, Adam
arrived just as she had finished drying her breakfast
dishes. After kissing her hello, he linked his hands
around her waist.

'Do you fancy going sailing this afternoon?' Intui-
tion told her his broad grin signified something special.
He did not wait for an answer. 'I'll pick you up from
the quay steps at one-thirty. Have you any oilskins?'
When she shook her head he brushed the matter aside.
'I expect Janet can lend you some.'

'Adam, whose boat are we——?' Realisation
dawned. 'You haven't——?'

'I most certainly have!' His smile widened. 'She's
called *Mary-Ann*. She's twenty-three feet long, seventy
years old and has the traditional wooden hull and gaff
rig. She's "proper 'andsome", according to Eddy
Trewin and the Treloar brothers, who checked her out

for me. She was built locally for the Glassons, and this is the first time she's been owned by anyone outside that family.'

'You rotten so-and-so!' Shelley hit him with the tea-towel. 'You never said a word.' Her heart gave its familiar kick as he laughed. Would she ever tire of looking at him, of hearing his voice, of learning to recognise all his nuances of expression and mood?

'I wanted it to be a surprise. Matt's had her in the yard. She's been scraped and repainted, her mast and bowsprit revarnished and her rigging replaced. This will be her first outing.'

'Then I'm honoured,' Shelley hugged him.

'No,' he said softly, 'it's she who is honoured.'

Shelley felt warmth suffuse her. How could she doubt he loved her? What were words, after all? She looked up at him. 'There's only one small problem.'

'Forget the shop this once.'

'It wasn't the shop.'

'You don't get seasick?' He looked horrified.

'No,' she grinned. 'But I've never crewed on a boat this size, though I'm willing to learn,' she added quickly. 'I just thought I'd better warn you. I won't be a lot of use.'

'I wouldn't say that.' He regarded her through half closed eyes. 'As a matter of fact, I have plans for you. But as far as a crew is concerned,' he went on before she could utter a word, 'Eddy and Janet Penrose, and Eddy's brother, Clive, are coming with us.' He held her close again, 'I'll see you later,' and kissed her even harder than usual.

When he'd gone, Shelley stood at the door for a moment, touching her lips with fingers that trembled slightly. There had been a pent-up force, a rigidly controlled excitement within Adam which she sensed was not entirely due to his pleasure over the boat. Some of it had transferred itself to her and she felt quivery inside. Her heart beat faster and her perception sharpened as anticipation tautened every nerve.

Warmly dressed in cords, shirt, thick sweater and gloves, Shelley pushed her arms into the oilskin jacket.

'There'll be room for the rest of us in there as well by the look of it,' Janet observed as Shelley turned the sleeves back before buttoning it up. After she had put both feet into one leg and pulled the waistband up to her chest, Shelley decided to abandon the trousers. Still giggling, she and Janet went down the steps to where the dinghy, with Adam at the oars, waited to row them out to where *Mary-Ann* tugged restlessly at her mooring on the choppy water.

The afternoon was fresh and sunny. A stiff breeze sent puff-ball clouds scudding across a clear blue sky. All around them, amid the sounds of shouted instructions, laughter, the ringing of wires and ropes against aluminium masts, and the slap of waves against hulls, other workboats were setting their sails and casting off, surging forward as wind filled canvas.

Shelley stood near the stern on the windward side, with Adam at the helm on one side and Janet on the other. Eddy and Clive hoisted the big mainsail, then set the jib and small triangular sail at the top of the mast.

Beneath Shelley's feet, the boat felt alive, leaping and dipping, shouldering the waves aside and heeling over as Adam held a tight course.

'Well, boy?' Eddy shouted to Adam above the hiss of wind and sea. 'Are us 'aving a trip round the bay like bleddy tourists, or are 'ee going to see what you bought 'ere?'

Adam's laugh was a deep-throated joyous burst of sound. 'That's some choice, Eddy.' His eyes sought Shelley's. He didn't need to speak. That one, slightly raised eyebrow was question enough. Was she nervous? Would she rather take it slow and easy? He was awaiting *her* decision.

Shelley glanced up at the mast head. The odd tingle

in her spine told her there was more at stake than a pleasant afternoon on the water. The sails were full and taut. They were approaching the start line of the workboat race that Adam had vowed to win. Ahead of them eight other workboats crossed and recrossed the line as they jostled for position. She brought her gaze back to his face. 'Go for it, Adam,' she said softly, smiling.

His eyes blazed, held hers an instant longer, then he looked at Eddy. 'OK, let's see what she can do.'

Clive and Eddy exchanged a grin and Eddy gave a satisfied nod. 'Right, my girl,' he slapped one calloused hand on to the gunwale, 'pick up your skirts.'

The starting gun boomed out and *Mary-Ann* swept over the line, creaming past three other boats which had overrun and had to turn back to re-start.

The next hour was, for Shelley, a breathless, exhilarating experience.

Adam drove the boat hard, making use of every ounce of wind and canvas. *Mary-Ann* sliced through the water like a knife through butter. Ahead and behind, the other workboats were strung out over the course. Eddy, who knew them all by the colours of their hulls, kept up a running commentary, occasionally shouting bits of information or advice to Adam about currents or fluctuations in the wind caused by coastal features.

Rounding the buoys produced a flurry of activity as Adam, edging in far closer than Shelley thought safe, pushed the helm hard over and the heavy boom swung to the opposite side. Clive and Eddy hauled the sheets in with a speed born of long practice, catching the wind again almost immediately, and *Mary-Ann* leapt forward on her new course.

Shelley's heart was in her mouth for much of the time as the boat flew along at an angle of forty-five degrees and the sparkling foam of their bow wave looked as if it might spill in over the lee rail.

'Only two ahead,' Eddy yelled. 'Watch out for the *Bess*. George'll cut across yer bows if 'e thinks you're getting too close.'

Adam nodded briefly, but held his course. The distance between the two boats was lessening every minute.

Shelley didn't catch what Adam shouted, but Eddy clearly did for, after exchanging a quick surprised glance with Clive, both men's faces split into huge grins. Eddy spat on his hands and rubbed them in delight.

'What's happening?' Shelley asked Janet.

'Mr Trelawney's going to take George on.'

Second by second, *Mary-Ann* was gaining. Shelley saw the other helmsman glance round then lean forward to yell and wave at his crew.

Janet nudged Shelley. 'Going to be some fun now,' she observed.

Only a few yards separated the boats. Shelley clutched at the rail and held her breath. She shot a quick look at Adam. His eyes were narrowed and his jaw set as his gaze flickered continuously from the mainsail to the boat ahead and back. But his hand on the tiller was rock-steady.

He caught her eye and winked. As a contact it lasted only a fraction of a second, but its effect on Shelley was stunning. It told her so much. Despite the battle between the two boats, despite his fierce concentration and the challenge he was clearly enjoying, *she* was uppermost in his mind.

'Right, boys!' Adam shouted.

Shelley gasped. The boat in front turned across their path. Her eyes shut tight as she waited for the crunch, Shelley didn't see what happened next, but she felt *Mary-Ann* hesitate, then jink sideways. As she opened her eyes, a roar went up from Eddy and Clive. Adam let out a great shout of laughter. *Mary-Ann* surged forward on the opposite side of their rivals who were working furiously to make up the lost ground.

Shelley and Janet were both waving and squealing with delight. The gun boomed again and *Mary-Ann* raced over the finish line in second place.

Shelley turned an ecstatic face to Adam and unable to contain her excitement, hugged his arm. He drew it free and lay it across her shoulders, holding her close.

'Remember that bet?'

She nodded.

'I'm claiming my prize.'

'But you didn't win,' she pointed out, pushing her wind-blown hair out of her eyes.

'This is my first race and I came second. Do you doubt I'll make first place before the season's over?' he challenged.

'A man of confidence,' she grinned up at him.

He gave a brief nod. 'Now, about my prize . . . '

'I should have had more sense than to bet against you.' Impulsively, she stood on tiptoe and kissed his cheek. 'Congratulations. I was scared stiff, but it was fantastically exciting. So what's it to be? I pay for a celebration dinner tonight?'

He motioned with his head for her to come closer, then brought his mouth down to her ear. 'Marry me, Rochelle.'

She jerked back as though she had been stung, wide-eyed, incredulous. She swallowed and attempted a faltering smile. 'Do you know, I thought you just asked——'

'You to marry me,' he finished. 'I did.' His voice roughened. 'Will you? Please?'

CHAPTER TEN

'THAT'S far too long to wait,' Adam growled, drawing the Daimler smoothly to a stop on the freshly gravelled drive.

Shelley laid her hand on his. 'I don't want to wait any more than you do,' she assured him, 'but surely a week——'

'Is far too long,' he repeated. 'We could get a special licence and be married within forty-eight hours.'

'Why the hurry, Adam?' Shelley asked softly, puzzled. 'What difference can a few more days make?'

Half turning in his seat, he seized her shoulders. Unaware of his strength, his grip was punishing; and his eyes glittered fiercely. 'I can't go on like this. It's tearing me apart. I want my ring on your finger and your body in my bed. I want to wake up beside you and know you'll be there to come to each night. I want to see your clothes in the wardrobe, your tooth-brush in the bathroom and your face across the table at breakfast——' He broke off. The light above the front door spilled on to the hard planes of his face. His expression was tormented, as though a battle was raging within him. 'I want you. Permanently,' he muttered harshly. 'I love you, Rochelle.'

'Oh, Adam,' she whispered, reaching up to touch his face. 'I've waited so long——' Her heart was too full and she caught her trembling lower lip between her teeth as tears of joy spilled over her lashes and slid down her cheeks.

He looked at her for a long moment, then leaned forward silently and licked them away with the tip of his tongue. As he kissed her mouth with exquisite tenderness, Shelley knew she would remember this moment as long as she lived. Independent, self-sufficient, it had cost Adam dearly to admit his emotional need for her. It was a treasure beyond price.

Slowly he released her, his eyes never leaving hers. 'We'd better go in.'

She nodded. Her heart was pounding and she was light-headed with happiness. This was what she had yearned for. Adam loved her. As tears threatened again she turned her head to look at the house. The scaffolding had gone and, in its coat of fresh paint, illuminated by the spotlights at the edge of the lawn, the house was serene and splendid.

'Of course, you'll need a car of your own,' Adam said suddenly.

Shelley jerked round. 'What?'

A grin softened his features. 'It's not another fiendish plot to undermine your independence. If anything, I'm increasing it. You see, much as I would enjoy driving you to your shop every morning—I'm assuming you intend to continue with your career?' She nodded quickly, her eyes shining. He gave a sigh of mock martyrdom. 'I guessed as much. The point is, I may not always be free to do so. With a car of your own the problem is solved.'

'Thank you,' she whispered huskily, and kissed him.

'It's my pleasure.' Though his tone was flippant, the look in his eyes tore at her heart. The barriers were finally down. He pointed to the spot her lips had just touched. 'Again.'

Laughing, she obliged, trying to convey how very much she loved him.

'Enough,' he grated a few minutes later, and with obvious reluctance, put her away from him. 'We really must go in.' He took the keys from the ignition.

Shelley picked up her evening bag. 'Why have we come here? Have you forgotten something?'

'No. But with so much to plan and discuss I thought we would be more comfortable here, and certainly more private.' He paused. 'Would you prefer to go somewhere else?'

Shelley shook her head. 'This is a lovely surprise.' She smiled up at him. 'It's been a day of lovely surprises.

Darkly handsome in his charcoal suit, his white shirt a startling contrast to his black hair and bronze skin, Adam raised her hand to his mouth and kissed her palm. 'It's not over yet,' he murmured, looking deep into her eyes.

A surge of excitement sent tingles down her spine and her pulses raced. Shelley took refuge in humour. 'You didn't cook dinner as well?'

'Don't mock,' he warned. 'My culinary expertise has been known to reduce trained chefs to tears.' He got out of the car. By the time she had opened her door, he was there. The touch of his hand on hers was electric. 'But tonight Mrs Tregenza stayed on to do it. I dropped her off on my way to collect you.' He steered her towards the front door. 'She wishes us every happiness and wants us to remember her sister Violet's girl.'

Puzzled, Shelley glanced at him. 'Why?'

'Apparently the young lady has just finished her training as a nanny and Mrs Tregenza is quite sure she would suit us perfectly.'

Shelley blushed and giggled. 'I'm very grateful for Mrs Tregenza's foresight, but I think I'd like you to myself for a year or two first.' Her voice softened. 'We have so much lost time to make up.'

'Rochelle, I—you——' Adam said thickly and, cupping her face, stroked her cheek with his thumb.

She caught her breath. What she saw in his eyes sent an exquisite thrill through her. 'It's all right,' she whispered, placing her hand over his. 'I understand.'

As he hung up her coat, Shelley glimpsed her

reflection in the hall mirror. Her tawny hair was piled on top of her head in soft, shining curls, and her slim-fitting dress of cream and gold silk-jersey lent her a sophistication that surprised and delighted her.

Loving and being loved changed a woman's whole life, she mused. In the few hours since Adam had proposed, she had felt herself more attractive, more feminine, more *complete*. This was how it was meant to be. They were two halves of a whole, each capable of functioning alone, but together——'We'll set the world on fire. Well, our world anyway,' she confided softly to her reflection.

'What was that?' Adam approached her.

Shelley turned towards him. 'How sad it is that it's taken three years apart to make us finally realise what we mean to each other.'

'No, Rochelle,' he was suddenly sombre, 'it has taken *you* three years. I have always known exactly what you mean to me.'

She grasped his hand. 'Oh, Adam,' her eyes filled with tears. 'I do love you.'

He smiled. 'Let's go in.' He cupped her elbow and led her towards the drawing-room. 'Have I told you how beautiful you look tonight?'

Radiating happiness, she tilted her head, smiling at him. 'Yes,' she admitted, 'but I think I could stand hearing it again.'

His grip tightened. 'You will,' he laughed. 'You will.' He opened the door.

Shelley froze, speechless. She glanced at Adam, whose broad smile revealed his complicity in the situation, then back at the couple.

Her father pushed himself out of the armchair, placed his half-empty glass on the low table, and stood up, uncharacteristically hesitant.

Her mother remained seated on the sofa, but beneath the immaculate coiffure and the flawless make-up, she was smiling.

'Rochelle, my dear.' Richard Barrington-Smythe started forward, his hands outstretched. 'You look wonderful. Life in this part of the world clearly suits you.'

Suddenly, Shelley saw past the urbanity and polish. She saw the sheen of perspiration on her father's forehead, and the way her mother ceaselessly turned the massive diamond on her third finger. Adam had been right. They were *nervous!* With that realisation came another. *She wasn't!* Shocked, surprised, but not *nervous.* A great weight slid from her shoulders.

Reaching out, she launched herself at her father, half laughing, half crying. 'Oh, Daddy, it's marvellous to see you again.'

Her father hugged her to him, unable to speak. Shelley saw her mother stand up and, gently breaking her father's embrace, put her arms around Celia, inhaling the familiar perfume, feeling her mother's bird-like fragility under her elegant, high-necked, full-sleeved black dress.

'But how——? Who——?' Shelley began.

'As soon as you had written to us,' her father explained, 'Adam also wrote, and between us we arranged this little surprise.'

Adam's grin confirmed what her father was saying. Then everyone started talking at once. Surreptitious tears were wiped away, news and gossip exchanged. Adam handed around drinks and at Shelley's insistence explained his part in the subterfuge. Then, with a quiet pride that brought yet another lump to Shelley's throat, he announced their impending wedding.

Shelley intercepted the glance her parents exchanged, but their delight was so obvious she put it down to surprise.

Adam steered them into the dining-room and expertly served the delicious meal Mrs Tregenza had prepared, while Shelley described to her parents her efforts to establish the Gallery and all that had happened since. They were by turns appalled, amused and admiring. Adam added his own comments, making Shelley blush when he recounted her initial reactions to his reappearance in her life. Later he reduced them all to helpless laughter with anecdotes concerning his battles with the various local authority departments.

After the meal, they returned to the drawing-room. Leaving Adam to build up the fire and her parents admiring the panther, Shelley went to make coffee.

Waiting for it to percolate, she gazed round the kitchen, admiring the way Adam had blended modern with traditional. She pictured herself cooking breakfast, starting a new life with him. Leaning against the oak breakfast-bar, she hugged herself and sighed, ecstatically happy. It had all come right. She and Adam were together again and nothing, *nothing,* would ever come between them. She was reunited with her parents, and re-established in her work. Life was wonderful.

Adam had poured a brandy for Richard and himself, and Cointreau for Shelley and her mother.

'The river bed has been causing problems with the foundations,' he was saying to Richard.

'What are these flats of yours going to look like?' Celia enquired, her fine-boned features thoughtful. Before Adam could reply she turned to her husband. 'You know, Richard, if Adam and Rochelle intend to remain down here, it might not be a bad idea for us to have a little pied-à-terre. We could always let it to our friends.'

'You don't need to buy a place,' Shelley smiled at her mother. 'You know you'd always be welcome here. Wouldn't they, Adam?'

'Of course.'

Celia's perfectly painted mouth tilted at the corners. 'That's very sweet of you, darling, but we value our privacy, too. We'd all get along much more happily *choosing* the time we spend together, rather than having it thrust upon us by sharing the same roof.'

'I think the flats would appeal to you, Celia,' Adam said. 'Perhaps you'd both like to see the plans?'

'Great idea,' Richard rubbed his hands together. 'Property's always a sound investment.'

'I'll fetch them,' Shelley offered, already on her feet. 'We need more coffee, anyway.' As she went out, Adam began to describe the difficulties encountered by his engineers. Watching him totally absorbed, Shelley felt an odd tug at her heart. Her dreams had become reality. Adam loved her.

Humming happily, she refilled the silver pot from the percolator. Opening the door to Adam's study, she pulled a face at the clutter of papers across the desk. As she reached beneath them for the rolled plan, the pot tilted and a few drips of coffee spilled on to the corner of an important-looking document. Hastily setting the pot down a safe distance away, Shelley hurried round the desk, snatching a tissue from her sleeve.

Carefully blotting the stain, she lifted the edge of the thick, cream-coloured paper with its Gothic letter-head and red seal, and breathed a sigh of relief. The coffee had gone no further. Replacing the document in its original position, her eye was caught by the sight of her own name.

Pushing aside the other papers half covering it, Shelley realised the document was a will. Her gaze flew to the top of the page. Nicholas Edward Arthur Trelawney.

Her life had been so chaotic since her return from holiday, she had had little time to mourn the old man who, in his own way, had been so kind to her. She stared at the document, remembering. Then the words began to penetrate her consciousness. Her attention sharpened and a puzzled frown drew her brows together.

She lifted the first sheet and began reading the one

attached to it. No longer aware of her surroundings, oblivious to the coffee growing cold on the far side of the desk, she read the paragraph twice. At first unable to comprehend, then unwilling to believe the evidence of her own eyes.

For a moment she felt physically sick as shock churned her stomach and drained the blood from her face.

She read the words yet again, mouthing them silently, each one a hammer blow smashing at the foundations of all she felt for Adam.

Nicholas had left the cottages and Gallery to Adam *on condition* he married Rochelle Louise Barrington-Smythe within six months of the date of Nicholas's death. If this condition was not met, ownership of all three cottages reverted to Shelley and Adam was bound to pay over to her the market value of the Gallery site.

Blindly, she felt for the leather swivel-chair and sank into it. Her legs had turned to water and refused to support her.

Was this will the real reason for his interest in her? Had his courtship been nothing but a charade? Did he want to marry her only as a means of acquiring the property?

No! She could not, would not, believe that.

Then why had he not told her about the will?

Snatches of memory tumbled through her mind. Adam watching her through the windows as she worked, showing her over his house that first time, helping her sandbag the cottage doors, and when she joked about artistic licence, warning her there would be no others, only him. His kisses had not lied. He had been by turns tender and passionate. He had wanted her.

Yet they had not made love.

Today he had asked her to marry him, and told her he loved her.

In that order.

No, Adam was not capable of such treachery and deceit.

Then why had he not told her about the will?

His reappearance in her life, his purchase of this house, his constant pursuit of her and alienation of her friends, his admiration of her work and urging that she end the feud with her parents, each memory carried both pleasure and pain. Taken alone, each was as light and bright as a snowflake, and appeared to have only *her* interest at its heart. But together their weight was a dark, suffocating burden.

Desperately she fought back. It could all be explained. It was *her* he wanted.

Then why had he held back even when, her shyness forgotten, she had shown him how much she wanted him? Surely that would have been the ultimate vengeance, had such been his intention? Or could it be he had feared becoming *genuinely* involved?

There was only one thing to do. *Run*, one half of her screamed silently. *Avoid more hurt, more lies.*

Ask him, believe in him, the other half whispered.

And if she was wrong? If the past weeks had been nothing more to him than a cynical means of getting what he wanted?

But what *did* he want? The property? Against his wealth, the value of the cottages and even the Gallery site was negligible.

Then *what*? The question echoed in her mind. For a long moment there was no answer. When it came, Shelley closed her eyes against a pain too great to bear. Had he intended to do what she had done? Walk out on her two days before the wedding?

Slumping forward over the desk, Shelley clutched her head in her hands.

With a click the door swung open. 'Can't you find——? Rochelle?' Adam's voice mirrored his sudden concern. Shelley heard his footsteps as he strode towards her. 'Is something wrong?'

Slowly, Shelley turned her head towards him. 'Yes.' It hurt to speak. Her throat was stiff with a grief too deep for tears. She had to know the truth but could not bear to ask.

His gaze fell from her face to the document in front of her and, as she watched, a spasm crossed his face, leaving it set in harsh, bitter lines.

'Stay here,' he ordered. 'I'll take your parents back to their hotel, then we'll talk.'

'I'd better see them.' Shelley stumbled to her feet. She felt as though she had aged twenty years in the past five minutes.

'No!' Adam was abrupt. 'One look at you and they'd imagine the worst.'

'And what would that be?' Her voice cracked. 'What could be worse?' She knew the raw pain was naked on her face.

Adam's features were a mask, his eyes icy-grey and opaque. He had retreated to somewhere inside himself and was not giving even the smallest clue to his thoughts or feelings. 'Stay here,' he repeated. 'I'll tell them the excitement has proved a little too much. You're lying down for a while and will see them tomorrow.'

'And you think they'll just accept that?'

'I'll make sure they do.' His terse reply held no doubt. He went to the door. Turning the handle he glanced back. 'If you leave while I'm gone,' he said quietly, 'I'll find you. I don't care if it takes an hour, a month or a year. I'll track you down, Rochelle.'

A shiver ran down her spine but she lifted her chin. 'You don't need to threaten me, Adam. I'm staying because *I* choose to.'

She watched him disappear. A few moments later she heard voices as her parents emerged into the hall. The front door closed. The house was silent.

Weak and shaky, Shelley opened the study door.

She hesitated, looking towards the front door. Then, resolutely, she crossed the hall into the drawing-room.

Chilled to her soul, she sat on the floor by the hearth and tossed another log from the basket into the flames. She had said she would stay. But did she have the strength to accept what he had to tell her? As the fire crackled, Shelley rubbed her arms and wondered if she woule ever be warm again.

The Daimler's engine purred and gravel crunched beneath the wheels as it pulled away.

How long would Adam be? Forty minutes? An hour? the front door slammed, making her start. A moment later, Adam strode in. The strain in his face faded as he saw her sitting beside the fire. He said nothing. Crossing to the drinks cabinet, he poured himself another brandy and tossed it down his throat as if it was water.

In that instant Shelley realised he was less confident, less in control than he appeared. It also came to her in a blinding flash that he had not really believed she would stay.

Paradoxically, she felt a wild surge of hope. Remaining where she was, not trusting her legs, she clasped her hands tightly to stop them from shaking.

'I loaned your father the car. He'll return it in the morning,' Adam announced staring into his empty glass. 'When you want to leave, I'll phone for a taxi.'

'I'm going nowhere until you've explained,' she said quietly. 'You owe me that, at least.'

He glanced down at her, then turned away. 'I thought——' his voice was hoarse, 'I expected——' He moved his shoulders in a helpless shrug, unable to go on.

'That I'd run away again?' Shelley supplied. 'I have to admit it occurred to me. But I can't. I have to know the truth, Adam, however much it——' She swallowed, digging her nails into the softness of her palms. 'Did you intend to jilt me?'

He whirled round, his eyes ablaze. 'What?' He looked dumbfounded.

'Tonight . . . ' Shelley's voice faded completely, She cleared her throat and started again. 'Tonight I realised for the first time, what *you* must have gone through when I walked out on you.'

The brandy glass slipped from his hand and fell on to the marble hearth, smashing into fragments, and making them both flinch.

Ignoring it, he bent and, seizing her shoulders, his fingers hard and bruising, he hauled her to her feet. 'And you thought I was planning to avenge myself by doing the same to you?'

'It seemed to make sense,' she whispered.

He shook her hard. 'What sort of man do you think I am, for God's sake?'

'Then why, Adam?' she cried. 'Why didn't you tell me about the will?'

'Because I was afraid!' The words were torn from him. 'I knew when I walked into the Gallery the day you got back from your holiday that I still loved you. Despite all that had happened, you were, and always would be, the only woman for me. My grandfather meant well, but I damned him to hell and back for his meddling. I wanted you back, Rochelle, but you had left me once. To get used to me being around you needed the one thing I had so little of—time. I knew that if you learned about the will you would never be quite sure which had mattered most to me.'

'Oh, Adam,' Shelley rubbed her temples, 'what a tangle we've both been in!'

He released her so suddenly that she had to grab the mantelpiece for support. 'Adam!' The cry was instinctive, without thought. It came straight from her heart. 'Don't leave me.'

He caught her neck in one hand. His eyes glittered and a muscle jerked spasmodically in his jaw. 'Leave you?' he grated. 'How can I leave you? You're my life. But you're like a wild bird, you need space, the freedom to spread your wings. I tried to cage you once and you flew away. I hated you,' his voice dropped, 'or thought I did.'

Shelley read in is eyes the reflection of her own anguish. Thank God she had stayed. She would never have known, never have understood.

'Wait here.' He walked out, returning moments later carrying a folded document which he held out to her. 'I intended giving you this the day we got married.'

Shelley opened the document with trembling fingers and scanned it swiftly. Wide-eyed, she looked up at him.

'Check the date,' he ordered. 'That deed was prepared the day after Nicholas's will was probated. The property is yours and has been for several weeks. I have merely been acting as your agent. You are now a wealthy woman in your own right, Rochelle.'

He stood before her, tall, unbending, his handsome features carefully expressionless. He had laid his pride and his heart at her feet. Now he waited.

Shelley sighed, a ragged tearing sound that combined joy, relief and sadness for the torment they had both suffered. There was so much still to be said, but it could wait. He loved her, that was all that mattered. Peace filled her and she smiled at him. 'As I said,' she bit her lip, 'a day full of lovely surprises.'

She watched the tension drain out of him. His mouth curved in a slow smile and lit his eyes with such love and tenderness that Shelley's heart skipped a beat. 'And as *I* said,' he took her hand, holding it in both of his, 'it's not over yet.'

Shelley dropped the document on to the low table and they walked together to the door. As Adam switched off the lights, Shelley glanced back. The firelight danced on the shards of broken glass, and on the panther, crouched above.

She met Adam's steady gaze. 'Ready?' he asked softly.

'Ready,' she smiled, and he led her up the wide, curving staircase.

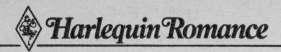
Harlequin Romance

Coming Next Month

Available in January wherever paperback books are sold, or through Harlequin Reader Service.

In the U.S.	In Canada
901 Fuhrmann Blvd.	P.O. Box 603
P.O. Box 1397	Fort Erie, Ontario
Buffalo, N.Y. 14240-1397	L2A 5X3

Six exciting series for you every month... from Harlequin

Harlequin Romance·
The series that started it all

Tender, captivating and heartwarming...
love stories that sweep you off to faraway places
and delight you with the magic of love.

◆

Harlequin Presents·
Powerful contemporary love stories...as individual as the women who read them

The No. 1 romance series...
exciting love stories for you, the woman of today...
a rare blend of passion and dramatic realism.

◆

Harlequin Superromance®
It's more than romance... it's Harlequin Superromance

A sophisticated, contemporary romance-fiction
series, providing you with a longer,
more involving read...a richer mix of complex plots,
realism and adventure.

Harlequin
American Romance™
Harlequin celebrates the American woman...

...by offering you romance stories written about American women, by American women for American women. This series offers you contemporary romances uniquely North American in flavor and appeal.

◆

Harlequin Temptation™
Passionate stories for today's woman

An exciting series of sensual, mature stories of love...dilemmas, choices, resolutions... all contemporary issues dealt with in a true-to-life fashion by some of your favorite authors.

◆

Harlequin Intrigue
Because romance can be quite an adventure

Harlequin Intrigue, an innovative series that blends the romance you expect... with the unexpected. Each story has an added element of intrigue that provides a new twist to the Harlequin tradition of romance excellence.

Harlequin Books·

PROD-A-2

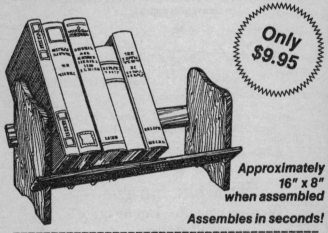

Harlequin
Intrigue

In October
Watch for the new look of

Harlequin Intrigue

...because romance can be quite an adventure!

Each time, Harlequin Intrigue brings you great stories, mixing a contemporary, sophisticated romance with the surprising twists and turns of a puzzler... romance with "something more."

Plus...
in next month's publications of Harlequin Intrigue we offer you the chance to win one of four mysterious and exciting weekends. Don't miss the opportunity! Read the October Harlequin Intrigues!

Coming Soon
from Harlequin...

GIFTS FROM THE HEART

**Watch for it
in February**